Dark Chapters: Pharaoh

The Egyptian Nightmare

Hannah MacFarlane

Also by the same author:
Fire by Night
The Silent Cord

© Hannah MacFarlane 2010
First published 2010
ISBN 978 1 84427 535 9

Scripture Union
207–209 Queensway, Bletchley, Milton Keynes, MK2 2EB
Email: info@scriptureunion.org.uk
Website: www.scriptureunion.org.uk

Scripture Union Australia
Locked Bag 2, Central Coast Business Centre, NSW 2252
Website: www.scriptureunion.org.au

Scripture Union USA
PO Box 987, Valley Forge, PA 19482
Website: www.scriptureunion.org

Scipture quotations taken from the New American Standard Bible®, copyright © 1960, 1962, 1963, 1968, 1971, 1972, 1973, 1975, 1977, 1995 by The Lockman Foundation. Used by permission. (www.lockman.org)

British Library Cataloguing-in-Publication Data
A catalogue record of this book is available from the British Library.

Printed and bound in the UK by CPI Bookmarque, Croydon, CR0 4TD

Cover design: GoBallistic

Scripture Union is an international charity working with churches in more than 130 countries, providing resources to bring the good news of Jesus Christ to children, young people and families and to encourage them to develop spiritually through the Bible and prayer.

As well as our network of volunteers, staff and associates who run holidays, church-based events and school Christian groups, we produce a wide range of publications and support those who use our resources through training programmes.

For Hope Church

PROLOGUE

Dudimose was not present to witness the final horrific insult unfolding.

A man cowers behind a statue of Pharaoh. Heart racing. Breathing hard. His eyes are wide. Alert. Scared. He hears pounding hooves reverberate from the colonnade, echoing inside his head. Sees chariot wheels spinning past at speed. He can smell his own fear. The temple has been infiltrated. He has managed to hide. Scrambled to safety as foreigners poured in and the reverent hush was shattered in a second. People run screaming. There's chaos. Noise. Fear. They don't know where to go or how to escape. The man watches a child scream for its mother – separated – alone and vulnerable. He longs with everything in him to help. The child is an easy target. But he can't move from his hiding place. There's too much risk to himself. He feels selfish. Cruel. Guilty even. He feels sick. His heart breaks. But his own survival is everything.

'*Psst.*'

The eerie voice startles the man. It is much too close. He turns slowly, thinking desperate thoughts the whole time. *Survive. Please just find a way to survive.* As he turns, bright sunlight glints into his eyes, reflected from the bronze tip of a sword. It blinds him. He squints and throws his hands to his eyes to shade them. Then the sword is pressing into his skin. Sharp. Cold. Dangerous. It's pointing at his throat. He doesn't dare move. The foreigner prolongs the moment. He has armour. And weapons. The man does not. He has nothing. His eyes are pleading. *Don't. Please don't.* It is a long, cruel wait. He thinks of his life. His ambitions. His loves. He thinks of that child screaming torturously. The man is close to tears. Then a sudden agonising pain tears through his body. Rips him apart. It's intense. Unbearable and all-consuming. His scream is silent. His vocal cords have been severed. His knees weaken. His vision blurs. Shadowy shapes swim around in front of his eyes. He reaches out, grasping at the air. His head is throbbing. He can't think. He staggers. The man collapses. His body slumps against the statue. His head cracks. He slides to the floor, smearing thick brilliant-red blood down the Pharaoh's solid stone calf muscle. Blood pools around him. He is gasping. Choking. Then silence. Darkness. Death.

Neither was Ibiya.

Deadly arrows whistle through the air. Worshippers run screaming. They scatter. Many flee towards the gate. The attackers' bows have a range like nothing they've ever witnessed before. They can't outrun the arrows. They are picked off one by one. Struck in the head. Or the back of the neck. They slump to the ground, pierced and bleeding. Others try to hide in the chapels of the gods. The sharpened daggers and swords of their pursuers follow them. They do not escape. They are stabbed. They are sliced. They are severed. Discarded where they die, body parts lay strewn around the square stone altars. One man tries to be a hero. He stands strong. But his defiance is hopeless. He is unarmed, untrained and unprepared. The people are efficiently massacred. Men are being slain. Women are callously murdered. Children slaughtered. One by one, their voices are silenced until finally the screaming ends. The pristine white wall is spattered with ruby red. Streams of blood flow across the floor. Glassy eyes stare up from the ground. Hollow. Lifeless. Cold empty symbols of the life they once held. Like the immense statues flanking the doorways. The power they represent has been much too easily overthrown.

They had been caught entirely off guard.

The sacred lake had been still earlier that day. Ceremonial calm had graced the avenue outside. Egyptians had arrived in droves to worship their gods in the early morning. Noblemen and servants, priests, farmers and scholars made their way together toward the great archway; the entrance to their new temple. Their purpose was the same; to collectively appease the gods of Egypt. To make a fresh start. They stared in awe of the beauty and strength of the new building. They had stopped to appreciate each detail. There were engraved records of Egypt's victories on the vast pylon, fascinating in their detail. Pennants quivered in the breeze at the top of tall cedar wood masts. The immaculately carved statues stood proudly in strategic locations. The people had pointed and whispered and gasped. They could not have suspected then what would happen. They remained happily oblivious. They did not know that this would be their only visit to this glorious place. They could not predict the torment that would tear through the temple. Destroying it. Destroying them.

The world's greatest civilisation was vulnerable and exposed. Egypt was defenceless.

The hostile foreigners regroup to survey their handiwork. They are victorious, but that alone is not enough. Their job is not done. With powerful blows of their axes, they attack the infrastructure of the building. They slash at the base of each column. The work is hard, but they are persistent. They grunt, sweating as they wield their tools until the thick cylindrical shafts topple and plummet to the ground, bringing down the narrow perimeter roof with a crash that resounds for miles around. They obliterate epic monuments, eradicate the many symbols of excellence and leave the sacred space in ruins. Great clouds of choking dust plume high into the air. Buried beneath mounds of huge stone fragments, lie its citizens. And its many treasures. The invaders have razed the temple to the ground.

A society that had already lost so much had now also lost its heart.

The destruction of the temple was an unnecessarily brutal display of power. An abomination. The insult was cruel. Before the invaders even arrived, Egypt had been reduced to a mere shadow of its former glory. The foreigners had seized power without striking a single blow. But they chose this brutality to make a point. This massacre and the burning of the city that followed were designed to send a clear message. The reign of the 13th Egyptian Dynasty was now over.

Dudimose had not been present to witness the final horrific insult unfolding. Neither had Ibiya. They had left the world's greatest civilisation weak and exposed to attack. They had also left it powerless to defend itself.

Egypt had just paid the price.

Part one

Authority

Chapter 1:

Pharaoh

Dudimose stood at the top of the flight of steps and surveyed the scene. This was his favourite place in the vast palace. Unlike the rest, this area was not adorned with gold or fine linens, there were no statues and the columns were not engraved with images or hieroglyphs. Despite this, it was here that Dudimose felt most relaxed and in control. The lack of elaborate decoration was naturally a deliberate choice. Nothing in the design of his palace was accidental. Indeed, he left nothing in his entire civilisation to chance. The combination of the plain steps, unadorned columns and simple square roof formed a perfect podium. Looking up from the courtyard below, the structure framed Dudimose, drawing attention to his youthful, muscular form, his fine garments and his elevated countenance. It emphasised his status. This was exactly as it should be, exactly as he had planned it, because this was exactly the view of himself he wanted to portray to his subjects. There were many grandiose statues and engraved images emphasising his best features throughout Egypt. But it was from this podium that Dudimose most often addressed his public and it was from the courtyard at the bottom of these steps that they most often saw their demigod.

But that was not what Dudimose loved most about this place. Better by far than knowing he was appearing to his best advantage was the spectacular view that this vantage point offered him. From here, Dudimose could see across the most affluent part of the city, his centre of power, to the wide expanse of the Nile. From where he now stood, down the steps, through the centre of the courtyard and out through the gates ran an imaginary axis. It continued through the entire city until it reached the Nile. Every street, building, monument, statue and temple that existed here had been built with reference to this axis, so that this, Dudimose's personal view of his world, was composed with perfect symmetry and balance. Every individual element of the view combined to complement the whole. Behind the sacred lakes rose great columns, which framed statues. These statues sat at the foot of altars. Those altars were flanked by chapels. A wide avenue led to a temple, beyond which significant residences stood in pleasing rows along the streets. All of this presented itself against the backdrop of the glistening water that flowed gracefully along this stretch of the River Nile and on the opposite bank Dudimose's finishing touch emerged fluidly from the flat sands; *his* pyramid. Everything that Dudimose saw when he stood at this spot belonged to him. Nothing had been designed or constructed that had not received his personal approval. His cartouche was everywhere. Standing here made Dudimose feel powerful. He was immensely proud of each achievement that made this city great. He took credit for realising this dream and it felt incredible to look out and remind himself of the magnificent world he ruled. But even more significant to him than the godlike feelings the scene conjured, was its overwhelming beauty.

Dudimose loved to wake early and arrive here before the heat of the day and his immense responsibilities began pressing in around him. At this time, he could be alone with his thoughts and this view. Alone, he could relax – and even smile. As he watched, the rising sun began to emerge from behind his pyramid. He held his breath as the first rays brushed the top of the glorious obelisk before it. That moment, when golden light illuminated the apex so that it appeared to glow, never failed to affect him. This morning, he released his breath in a slow, satisfied sigh. He knew that within minutes the ripples of the Nile would be glistening and the statue of a falcon in flight standing before the most prominent altar would be backlit, cast into dramatic silhouette. Soon after that, the city would awaken, and the day's responsibilities would begin. He lingered, determined to make the most of these last few moments of peace.

Dudimose was also hoping to defer one particular responsibility a little longer. He knew that some time in the future, his son would take his place on this spot, presiding over all the business of Egypt. His own eventual demise was as inevitable as the setting of the sun. Even the great Pharaoh of Egypt is mortal, after all. At that time, his son would rise into this position of great privilege and power like the sun now rising into the sky above him. There was so much for Dudimose to teach him before then. Not only were there general principals of governance, effective command of an army, understanding of construction and religious protocol, but also the less tangible qualities of a fine leader. Amongst these, he counted creating and maintaining a public persona, the art of diplomacy, an ability to inspire trust and increase morale, strength of character and wisdom. Long ago, he had appointed the beginning of his son's thirteenth year to commence these tasks. Though he knew that time had now arrived, Dudimose's heart sank at the thought of burdening his cherished firstborn son with the same constant weight he endured daily for his position. The image of Ibiya's carefree smile came into his mind. As he thought of what he was about to do, he saw the sparkle of his son's eyes dim and his infectious smile fade until his face grew solemn and inexpressive. Though it was only in his imagination, Dudimose's heir had altered and it saddened him.

Chapter 2:

Pharaoh's heir

'Well?'

Dad's eyes were sharp and probing. I shuffled a little and shifted my gaze from his solemn face to the man beside him. Though we had never had any dealings, I knew him well by sight. He fixed his eyes intently on me, waiting for my response. But I had no idea what I was expected to say; I cleared my throat and tried to look as though I was considering the question. My mind was blank. I was intensely aware of how hot it was and all I could think about was why suddenly my opinion mattered so much. *Concentrate*, I told myself. I looked back to my father, hoping for some clue in his expression. Some idea of what he expected from me. Scanning his features, I read nothing. In place of his warm smile and the glint in his eye that usually welcomed my interruptions, there was only a businesslike blank. I'd seen it before, of course, but never, as far as I remembered, had he looked this way at *me*. It was making me very uncomfortable.

'Shall we walk, Father? The colonnade would offer a little shade, or...' He raised one eyebrow a little. It was barely noticeable. Just enough to show me that he was still waiting and that my answer was now overdue. I hesitated.

'Certainly. I would be glad of the opportunity – after I have heard your thoughts.' His voice was calm and gracious and yet unambiguous. He had made his point. After. This assured manner was typical of my father. He was a man both comfortable with his status and fully expecting to be obeyed. Totally unlike me. I'd often wondered how I'd ever follow his act. I was horribly uncomfortable sharing my thoughts and only ever expected to be laughed at. But, he was giving me no choice but to speak out. I took a deep breath. If I was being honest, I did have an opinion. I just wasn't at all sure it was the 'right' one.

'I think the plans are ambitious.' I began, searching his face for approval. 'This is certainly bigger than anything you've undertaken so far and for that alone you would gain the public's admiration.' I was skirting the issue. 'It is a beautiful structure and would be perfectly placed.' He knew that already. I took another deep breath. 'And yet, I wonder if...' did I dare to say what was really on my mind? He seemed to want to know my opinion, but I was still unsure whether this was just a part of the great Pharaoh act. Was there a script he expected me to follow? I looked from one to the other, meeting their experienced eyes. In the next moment, I would either take one small step closer to gaining their respect or I would simply confirm my own stupidity. I squirmed under the pressure. Well, if there was a script, I certainly hadn't been given it. So 'I wonder if it's a little... unimaginative', I blurted. No response. 'It's bigger and bolder, yes, but it doesn't bring anything new.' The man, the top architect in all of Egypt, looked uncertainly at my father, waiting for a reaction. There wasn't one; not a discernible one anyway. He simply inclined his head slightly and continued to give me his full attention. I took that as my cue to go on, painfully aware that I could be prematurely constructing my own tomb. 'The columns, the pylons, the engravings... you've used them all before. The city is plagued with structures in this exact style. Personally, Father, I would prefer to see you bringing change to Egypt. That's how greatness is built.'

'The greatness of Egypt is already established,' the architect interjected. 'With respect, I was commissioned to pay tribute to your father with a design that heralds his achievements.'

Oh, help. I'd upset the architect now. Dad's favourite architect. Egypt's best. 'I understand. Your design certainly achieves those things. But...' What should I say? 'In my opinion...' There was nothing interesting or new in the design and I did believe that I was right; a building so significant *should* break new ground. With a deep breath, I looked up from my feet and addressed the architect directly. 'Egypt should not be allowed to stagnate. By building a memorial to Egypt, you might as well be declaring it dead. To be alive is to change and develop. We must offer something new. This is how we'll ensure that Egypt's greatness continues…' My heart was racing. I was actually quite excited by the idea that I could have something new and valuable to contribute to these plans. I met my father's eyes. Though they were professionally inexpressive, I knew I had made him think. When he asked my opinion, he could not have expected this from me. I'm certain he had believed his firstborn would meekly support his own views. But was he pleased, or cross? I couldn't tell. I was afraid it was cross. I turned towards him and lowered my voice, 'Father, you must not allow yourself to become inflexible now.'

Nothing more was said after that. Father gave a polite nod in my direction before dismissing his architect. I was left to wonder whether I had in fact said something extremely stupid – or whether I'd overstepped the line. The one that divided the forgivable, naïve mistakes, from the unforgivable, colossal, insulting errors of judgement. Had I insulted him? I feared I had. Would my father ever trust me again?

Chapter 3:

Slaves

Looking out from his haven at the top of the steps, Dudimose was glad of a few moments' peace. He had offered his firstborn some time away from his watchful eye and instruction to relax in whichever way he chose, and Dudimose was taking the opportunity to do the same. This particular morning had been, if anything, busier than usual. It had begun with that most interesting of meetings with his architect and had continued in much the same vein. He had conducted supervisory meetings with each of his advisors and second-in-commands in turn, made decisions numbering into the double figures and on top of all that, today's tasks had included the monthly changeover of lay priests. Taking into account that Ibiya had accompanied him throughout, at his own request, to begin training, Dudimose had also felt obliged to deliver a commentary; this consisted of a mixture of facts, explanation and opinion, though he had tried hard to keep the element of opinion to a minimum. He understood that, however strongly he believed that his years of experience had honed his own judgement to near perfection, his son must learn to think through matters for himself if he too was to become a Pharaoh of great stature.

Dudimose rubbed his temples and allowed himself to breathe. Overall, he judged that the morning had been successful. Though he had certainly not expected Ibiya to begin with such an assured attack on his architectural preferences, he did not mind. He laughed aloud now as he remembered his son's words, 'You must not allow yourself to become inflexible'. *Inflexible!* Was that really how his own flesh and blood perceived him? Of course, Dudimose never allowed himself to change direction with the wind – that would leave Egypt a chaotic mess – and the role required a certain focused determination, but he was by no means averse to change. He felt certain of that. He put it to the back of his mind and continued his personal re-examination of the morning's events.

★ ★ ★

'Those who have served in the temples of the gods and goddesses of Egypt over the past month have served well. The needs of each of our deities have been satisfactorily met and, as a result, no problems have arisen during your period of service. Egypt remains prosperous and healthy. For that, I thank you. You may return now to your respective families where you will find I have generously compensated you for your efforts.

You will continue in your usual employment for a period of three months, after which I will once again summon you to your priestly duties.'

Dudimose stood on his podium, addressing a crowded but reverent courtyard. He was presiding over the monthly changeover of lay priests. On this occasion, the task did not require the selection of any new candidates for the position; all were experienced in the role, and yet Dudimose proceeded with the ceremonious handover in full. In part, he wanted Ibiya to witness the tedium of his future role, along with the thrill of power in decision-making; but it was not only that. This issue was too important to leave to chance. The whole of Egypt, himself included, were at the mercy of the gods. Dudimose knew that for all his meticulous planning and efficient control of his territory, if the all-seeing-and-knowing gods were unhappy they could – and would – undermine everything he had striven for in an instant. And that would be unthinkably bad for him.

Dudimose paused while the dismissed priests dispersed and those remaining moved forwards. With a gesture, he silenced the courtyard and signalled for his son to step forward before continuing.

'Those who remain are to begin service in the temples for a period of one month from today. Your duties will be as follows.' He nodded to his son to begin.

'Each morning, you... you will break the seal to the sacred area of the temple. Using the torch to approach the statue, you will immediately say prayers and light incense. After this, you are to wash and dress the statue and place jewels upon it.' Ibiya hesitated a little, trying to recall the duties. 'Make offerings of food and drink and sing hymns. In addition, you are to ensure that worshippers remain at the gate to pray. Allow nobody but yourself into the sacred area. In the evening, when you leave, you will back out, sweeping away your footprints as you go. Finally, you will seal the area for the night.' He was gaining in confidence as he observed the rapt attention the crowd were paying to his words. 'With regard to your personal hygiene, you will shave your head and body daily, take cold baths at regular intervals throughout the day and wear clothes made only of linen.' Dudimose gave another polite nod and his son stepped back.

'I would like to stress to you all the importance of fulfilling these duties exactly as they have been set out for you. Egypt's well-being depends on the goodwill of all the gods and goddesses. Negligence or deliberate refusal to comply with these instructions will incur their wrath and cause harmful imbalance to our society. This is unacceptable. Just as I generously compensate those who serve well, I will punish severely those who do not. You may now begin your duties.'

★ ★ ★

Yes, Dudimose was pleased. He gave a satisfied nod as he loafed around his podium. Ibiya had been concise and clear, a little quiet perhaps, but audible. For a first public address, it was more than adequate. And that was exactly what he would tell him this afternoon. On the subject of those building plans, however, Dudimose was at a loss for what to say. He personally had been thrilled with the architect's work and enamoured with the design. It would have received his seal of approval on the spot, were it not for his son's observations. Could it really be bigger and better, but tiresome at the same time? Was that dichotomy possible? He was still mulling over this question when his thoughts were interrupted by the arrival of two figures in the courtyard below. He stopped ambling and drew himself up, presenting his visitors with the standard impenetrable Pharaoh Façade. As he took in the appearance of these two non-Egyptian men, hurried footsteps approached him. Without turning, Dudimose calmly admonished the young court attendant.

'Do not rush in my presence.' The scampering immediately halted. The child gave a deferential bow.

'I apologise Pharaoh, I...'

'They will wait. This meeting will begin when I am ready. Now tell me, who are these men?' The attendant slowly straightened himself and addressed Pharaoh.

'Their names are Moses and Aaron. They are Israelites. They bring a message.'

Dudimose sighed. He rolled his eyes. Israelites. What complaint did they bring now? He had little time for this sub-population of whinging slaves. For a nation who did not worship his gods or acknowledge his laws, managing them took up far too much of his valuable time. There was, unfortunately, some history. He wasn't clear on all the details, but he did know that a previous, clearly delusional, Pharaoh had granted them some land and some privileges and as a result they had thrived, increased greatly in number and become a serious potential threat to Egypt. Egypt was extraordinarily well defended, but if it came under attack and the Israelites chose to join forces with the enemy, purely because of their numbers, the result would be catastrophic. When he had died, the succeeding Pharaoh, his forerunner, had seen the power they held and made many efforts to mitigate the effects of the promises. He had succeeded in reducing the Israelites to servants of Egypt if not, despite drastic policy, decreasing their overall numbers. Now Dudimose had become Pharaoh, inherited power over Egypt, and continued faithfully in the mission to remove the threat. He could not rid the land of Israelites because of the covenant, but he had at least continued to increase their labour and make use of them. If they were going to reside in *his* Egypt, they would have to earn that privilege. The bricks they produced had built half of Egypt as it now stood. Still, they moaned too loudly, and too often. It bored him.

'Bring my son. He should witness this.' The attendant nodded once and was gone. Dudimose stood his ground, asserting his control over the situation by looking down on these intruders, enjoying making them squirm a little. He would descend to the courtyard to hear them when Ibiya arrived and not before. In the meantime, they could wait.

Chapter 4:

Request

I arrive to find my father on his podium, drawn up to full height and exuding dominance. The two men have turned away from the heat of his glare and are conferring in hushed tones in the sun-parched courtyard below. Knowing my father's opinion of Israelites, I feel a little sorry for them. This meeting will not be made comfortable. Or come anywhere close to achieving whatever purpose they have in mind. The only thing in question is how long Pharaoh will toy with them and draw out the discussion. He begins speaking as I approach, but all the time continues staring impersonally at the citizens he considers second-rate. This is just one of the tactics he uses to gain psychological advantage. He has many. And he is master of them all.

'Son, our duties have resumed sooner than I anticipated.' He then speaks much louder than necessary. 'I'm afraid these men have interrupted your leisure. And my mood is spoiled.'

I reply softly. 'Then let us begin the meeting, Father, and deal quickly with the matter, whatever it is.'

'Not so hasty.' My father looks sideways at me and I think perhaps there's a glint of humour in his eyes. 'These are Israelites. Slaves. They can wait.'

'For what?'

'They can just wait.' I don't know what to say to this, but it doesn't make sense to me. If the intrusion is unwelcome, surely it's best to get it over with. Why prolong things? I must look as confused as I feel because my father launches into an account that doubles as a lecture. 'Ibiya, these people are parasites. They are only here because of a heinous mistake in judgement made by one of my predecessors. Never forget that. They do not truly belong. There are too many of them, they are too strong and they are a threat to Egypt. They must not be allowed to control us.'

'But what about Joseph...?' As I say it, I know that my question will not go down well, but I can't help feeling uncomfortable about my father's firmly fixed opposition to these people. They are, after all, humans like the rest of us. And, the way I understand it, they earned their right to live here. Joseph is something of a legend here: interpreter of dreams, provider in time of famine, advisor to a Pharaoh. It is met with silence. He's ignoring it. Another tactic and this time I'm on the receiving end. 'He saved Egypt from famine. We wouldn't be here...'

'Apparently that is true. And yes, if so, he earned our thanks. But there is a principle. In such cases it is appropriate to give official thanks, respect; a reward even. But it is never a good idea to give away power. Never. *That* is where the fool-of-a-Pharaoh made his mistake. *That* is what we are still paying for. Don't ever forget that.'

'No, Father.' He's riled so I don't push it any further. He does make a good point, I suppose. Power must be protected. You can't just go round giving it away and still expect to maintain any sort of control. But he's also wrong. Personally, I'm not so sure it's Egypt that is paying for this so-called mistake. From what I remember of the situation, Israel have done more than enough to compensate Egypt for their presence here, and suffered more than anyone should ever...

'Now.' He interrupts my thoughts as if sensing that they are offensive to his own. 'I'm ready now. Let's meet these Israelite pests. But don't forget what I have told you.'

We walk deliberately down the steps. I keep a few steps behind my father out of deference, but also with the effect of distancing myself a little from what is about to happen. He stops a little way in front of the visitors and looks at them expectantly. He doesn't say a word to them. I suppose that's also part of his power game. He is still drawn up to his full height, chin up, eyebrows raised ever so slightly in a challenge. Everything about him seems to declare, 'nothing you could say would justify this abuse of my valuable time'.

The older of the two men shuffles uncomfortably. My father remains aloof. The younger steps forward, but then seems to think better of it and looks down at the floor. My father still calmly remains aloof. I wonder how long this stand-off will continue. I shift my weight carefully, trying to blend into the background. The older man looks at me and then my father. I think he's going to speak, but he doesn't. He looks back to me instead, a little pathetically. I incline my head and give a tiny nod of encouragement, hoping my father doesn't notice. *Go on, go ahead – speak.*

'Pharaoh Dudimose. Prince Ibiya.' He clears his throat and gives a little bow. His companion does the same. 'Pharaoh...' He seems unsure how to begin.

'Moses. Aaron.'

'Pharaoh...' Moses looks helplessly at Aaron, who steps forward, closer to Moses. I am stunned as Moses leans over and whispers to Aaron. The two do not seem prepared for this meeting and Moses, in particular, seems noticeably uncomfortable to be here. Finally, Aaron straightens himself and speaks.

'Thus says the Lord, the God of Israel, "Let my people go that they may celebrate a feast to me in the wilderness."' There's a moment of silence that feels much longer than it really is. It's one of those moments where everyone, me included, wishes they were somewhere, anywhere else. Pharaoh is the only one unfazed. He takes his time before responding icily.

'Who is "the Lord" that I should obey his voice to let Israel go?' Then he raises his voice so that it resounds powerfully through the courtyard. 'I do not know the Lord!' He turns and begins to climb the steps. As he passes me, somewhat shocked at how quickly he has dismissed the matter, he adds an afterthought. '…and besides, I will Not. Let. Israel. Go.' The last four words are heavily emphasised by his staccato and there is no doubt that he means it. I exhale slowly. Though he detests the Israelites, he still believes intrinsically that, like everything else in Egypt, they belong to him. As long as they are still useful to him, he will not part with them. And it's all part of his show of power. All these two men have done today is to give him an opportunity for another demonstration of that. I am about to turn away when Aaron speaks again. I don't know many people who would have the courage to do that once my father had made it clear that his meeting was over. I certainly wouldn't. It stuns me, gaining my full attention on impact. I am a captive audience.

'The God of the Hebrews has met with us.' I really don't want to see how this ends, but at the same time I can't convince myself to look away. 'Please, let us go a three days' journey into the wilderness that we may sacrifice to the Lord our God, otherwise he will fall upon us with pestilence or with the sword.' I am riveted to the scene.

My father is angered. This time, he does not hide his emotion behind the Pharaoh mask. He turns and addresses the Israelites with the full force of his wrath. 'Moses and Aaron, why do you draw the people away from their work? Get *back* to your labours!' They look taken aback, but do not move. 'Look, the people of the land are now many, and *you* would have them cease from their labours!' With that, he stomps up the steps and disappears.

I stood reflecting as I watched Moses and Aaron commiserate with one another and make their way out of Pharaoh's courtyard. As predicted, the meeting had been made difficult for them and they had not been granted their request. That didn't really shock me. What did surprise me though, was the manner in which my father ended the meeting. It was completely unlike him. Very un-Pharaoh-esque. Stomping? Raising his voice? These men had hit a nerve. But why? They had brought a straightforward request, which warranted only a straightforward refusal from Pharaoh. So what could have upset my father so deeply to shake his city-wall-thick composure? I'm still thinking about his abrupt manner when I realise I am now standing in an empty courtyard. I turn and walk – without stomping – up the steps.

Chapter 5:

Refusal

'Father, can we…' when he looks up, he seems a little distracted. I've interrupted his thoughts. 'Can we talk?' I finish.

I wait for a response, which only comes in my father's usual measured time. He shakes off the glazed look and gestures for me to join him.

'What is it, son? It's been a long day.'

'I know, Father. I know. Would you prefer we leave it until…'

'No, no. Tomorrow will bring more business, more responsibility and more pressure. You must learn to use these rare moments of quiet to process your own reflections. There are few of them and we cannot afford to waste the opportunity. Come.' He smiles at me and in that second I return to being his son. All week he's looked at me like an apprentice; we've talked in businesslike tones and discussed endless official topics. Now, as I'd hoped, I can relax with my dad. This is much more comfortable and natural for me and makes what I've come to ask much easier. I feel the tension draining away as my muscles ease. 'What's on your mind, Ibiya?'

'I've been looking at some records today, Dad. I couldn't help thinking, at that meeting...'

'With my architect?'

'...the name was familiar. Moses. I couldn't work out why I recognised it.'

My father is a good listener when he chooses to be. And now, although his eyes are piercing me, he's choosing not to interrupt. I breathe deeply. With relief, I think. Or maybe to prepare myself. He's allowing me to get this off my chest and I really need that.

'He grew up here, didn't he? In the palace.'

This time I need an answer. I want my father to acknowledge what I've discovered. I want him to admit what he hadn't told me before we went into that meeting. I need to understand the way he acted.

'No. Not here. This palace is my creation.' He pauses to look hard at me, then consents, 'But one much like it, yes.'

'So, he's a lot like me?'

'A prince of Egypt?'

'Yes.'

'No, Ibiya. Far from it. Moses was brought up by the daughter of the Pharaoh. He lived here – as our attendants and servants do – but he would not have been party to the workings of the palace as you have been, or shared the immense privileges of the family.'

I'm not convinced. 'I cannot believe that he lived in the palace as a servant. The pharaoh's daughter would not have allowed…'

'You're right. Of course. But I still maintain that he would have been kept distanced from the family. She must have known he was an Israelite. She took pity on him, gave him a comfortable life, educated him, but… he was not – *is not* – one of us, Ibiya. Don't forget that. You're not like him. *He* is not like you.'

'She raised him as her own; it says that here.' I hold out the papyrus. My father doesn't take it. He glares at me. The mood is changing. How long will his patience with me hold out? I need to keep him with me a little longer.

'Yes – as *her* own. You're right. But not everyone accepted him. Pharaoh found out he was a Hebrew; that he'd escaped the order…'

'The infanticide order? The one which allowed him to kill innocent babies, just for…'

'…and sought to have him killed the instant he made his first mistake. How he must have waited for that moment.' I notice the way my father seems to identify with this pharaoh and squirm inwardly.

'Dad, could that be me? If I acted against you. For the sake of Egypt, would you ever…' I trail off, but my father understands where I'm going. He takes my face in his hands and looks me in the eye.

'You have not heard what I have been saying, son. You belong. You are my heir.' He enfolds me in his arms and holds me close. He speaks softly in my ear. 'Moses was – and still is – an imposter here, like the rest of the Israelites. You could not be more different, Ibiya. My son.' He lets that sink in fully. 'Tell me, why is this on your mind?'

'The meeting, Father. You treated him harshly.'

He chuckles, actually out loud. That irritates me. We'd been talking as equals. Now, I'm back in my place. Just like that.

'You have to be tougher, Ibiya. You can't let a swarm of slaves bother you. There are far more important things to think about here.'

'Dad, I can't forget it. They came in deference: politely, with a simple request. Why be so dismissive? So inflexible?'

'Inflexible.' He repeats it slowly. 'That word again? Is that really what you think of me, Ibiya? You have so much to learn. Deference? A simple request? They take me for a fool. Israelites make up most of our workforce. We need them here. Tell me; do you really believe that if we let them go, they'd willingly come back? We would never see them again!'

'Perhaps if you treated them better, they would come back.' I'm finding it harder to keep my voice in check. It wobbles with my frustration. Dad is not proving to be as open to listening to my viewpoint on this topic as he'd like me to believe.

'They're not the only population of slaves in Egypt, Ibiya. Many groups serve us here. It's not a big issue.'

'But that's exactly my point. All the others are treated decently. I still don't understand why your approach to Israel is so much harsher.'

'I admire your persistence, son, but you're going to have to learn when to...'

'You're avoiding my point, Dad.' I am quiet, calm, but insistent. I've been observing the master of this kind of assertiveness all week. He looks at me now. Behind his annoyance, there's a glimpse of respect in his eyes. I've learned something. I get the impression that he's now weighing up how best to manage me. I'm not a child any more, but not yet his equal either.

'You want to understand my policy, Ibiya? Is that it? The Israelites have land here. Land is equivalent to power. Historically, the harder we have worked them and the more we've tried to control them, the stronger they've become and the bigger they've grown. They multiply like flies! They need to be broken before they break us. I want to be the one to find their breaking point, Ibiya. And Egypt will remember me for it.'

I don't respond. What can you say in the face of such misplaced determination? I came intending to get my usually reasonable father to re-examine his views of the slaves. Now, eyes closed and head hanging, I reflect that I've only strengthened his existing belief. But the worst is still to come and the force of it takes me completely by surprise.

'Ibiya. You've helped me clarify this matter in my own mind. Thank you.' I hardly dare ask.

'I don't understand, Father. What have I clarified?' He smiles.

'I have already stepped up my campaign against this swarm of undermining locusts to prevent them challenging and compromising my position any further. You have confirmed for me my wisdom in doing so. Earlier today, I took the step of removing the daily supply of straw from the Israelite slaves. Their quota for the production of bricks for our building projects remains unchanged. Now though, they will have to source their own straw for this purpose. This will have the effect of increasing their labour. They will have no more time for laziness and indulging in plots and schemes against me. Never again will they take me for a fool. You watch – you'll see that what I have said is true.' I nod in defeat. What else can I do?

'And Ibiya, I'm finished thinking about this. Tomorrow we'll return to the infinitely more important topic of architecture.'

Chapter 6:

Moses

Moses left the court of Pharaoh with his head hanging in defeat. He was confused. Why had God picked him for this task? His thoughts drifted painfully back to his peaceful life in Midian. His days spent in the pasture looking after his father-in-law's flock; simple pleasures, simple concerns. Whole weeks and months would pass in uneventful bliss. When he'd fled Egypt in fear of his life he had no thought of ever returning. Now he was regretting that he had.

His heart felt heavy. He kicked at the ground and wished that he'd never seen that flaming bush. If only he'd taken the flock east and kept them on the lower, flatter ground that day. Then he wouldn't be here now. Why had he chosen the mountain? Moses lamented his choice and his curiosity too. He could have carried on walking when he'd seen the bush on fire. He'd only stopped to watch the flames dancing around for a second or two, captivated momentarily by their beauty and power, mesmerised by the pattern. If only he hadn't allowed himself to be distracted. But he had. It was then he'd spotted the oddity that had drawn him closer; the lack of withering leaves, blackening branches or rising ash that would ordinarily accompany a bush fire. Then he'd noticed that the fire didn't spread. It struck him that it was contained. At that point he'd known it was something special.

He'd been right. God was there, talking directly to him from a bush in the middle of nowhere. It was one of the more surreal moments of his life and he could list a few. God had told Moses about Israel's oppression in Egypt and his plan to free them. All the while, Moses had stood barefoot, half turned away to keep his face hidden and making sure to keep his distance from the holy ground. He had felt stupid and self-conscious but forced himself to concentrate on the message. Moses couldn't decide quite how he should act, but the discomfort was just about bearable. Until the moment God had said, 'I will send you to Pharaoh, so that you may bring my people, the sons of Israel, out of Egypt'. It hit him like a stone from a sling. He hadn't seen it coming, and it changed everything.

He recalled his response word for word. It was etched into his memory. 'Who am I, that I should go to Pharaoh and that I should bring the sons of Israel out of Egypt?' He'd been right. He wasn't up to this job. Yes, Israel's elders had listened, but they'd had nothing to lose. They needed to hope and they'd put that hope in Moses. Pharaoh, well... Pharaoh was a different matter. Moses knew he must appear foolish and worthless to the King of Egypt. He'd known all along he wasn't up to the task.

A tear formed in his eye as he wondered again what he was going to say to the elders now. How could he tell them he'd built up their hopes only to disappoint them? How could he tell them he'd failed?

As he wiped away the tear with a sigh that seemed to originate deep within his heart, a scary thought occurred to him that made him stop wallowing for a moment. He hadn't understood it at the time. He wasn't sure he did now, but God had predicted this, hadn't he? He'd known this was going to happen; 'The king of Egypt will not permit you to go, except under compulsion.' What had he meant 'under compulsion'? That was ominous. Moses' heart rate increased with the thought. He didn't know what it meant and in that moment he realised that, whether he wanted to or not, he was going to find out. He was right at the centre of this plan. God had put him there and there wasn't an easy way out. He wiped the sweat from the palms of his hands and shook his head, trying to think clearly. He squeezed his eyes tightly shut, willing the confusion to go away. When he opened them a moment later, three large men stood around him. Moses recognised them as supervisors over the workers. He also recognised the expression they wore; anger exuded from their furrowed brows, narrowed eyes and set grimaces. Before he could formulate words to speak, they launched their attack.

'May the Lord look upon you and judge you,' the first began in a quiet and controlled manner. Moses was unprepared for this, but the next was quick to follow. His manner was more agitated.

'You have made us odious in Pharaoh's sight and in the sight of his servants!'

The third just glared threateningly. Moses avoided meeting his eyes. He didn't want to risk provoking him. He was assessing how best to respond, when the first speaker concluded the proceedings. 'You have put a sword in their hand to kill us.' And with that parting blow, they walked away, leaving Moses even more bewildered than before.

Moses watched them storm away before sinking to his knees in despair. He felt so ill-equipped to deal with this onslaught. He was here to help these people and he'd only managed to make everything worse – much, much worse. In desperation he yelled at the sky, the agony welling up from inside. 'O Lord, why? Why have you brought harm to this people? Why did you ever send *me*? Ever since I came to Pharaoh to speak in your name, he has done harm to this people. And you... you have not delivered your people at all!'

Part two

Authority challenged

Chapter 7:

A show of power

'Prove it to me!' Dudimose challenged.

Aaron forcefully flung his crude staff down to the ground. It was large and heavy and clattered loudly. The echoes it generated, as it jerked and wobbled, resounded from the colonnades. Everyone watched closely as the staff rocked randomly into eventual silence. A long moment passed. The staff lay motionless. The blunt, flat base lay still at Moses' feet with the smooth rounded top end pointing toward Dudimose. Moses held his breath. Aaron closed his eyes. Nobody moved until the final echo had died away. Then Dudimose let out a long derogatory laugh which broke the silence. He raised a scornful eyebrow and shook his head. He had just witnessed a total failure! They had not been able to produce a demonstration. Not even a basic sign. Now perhaps he would hear the end of their snivelling request. Their god has no power! He turned to leave.

In that moment, everything changed. The atmosphere became tense. Dudimose felt an ominous shiver run down his spine. He turned back and looked down at the immobile staff. He couldn't help it. His eyes were responding to something outside of himself, pulling against his will. Dudimose didn't like the sensation at all. His laugh and the confident smile faded. He strained to move his eyes away – to regain control – but they fixated on the lump of wood. Dudimose had no choice but to watch as the blunt end stretched itself slowly and narrowed into a tapered point, like some sort of crude spear. The spherical top stretched too and a narrow slit appeared, splitting the now flattened oval horizontally in two. And it grew. The staff grew longer and longer. Dudimose didn't blink. He didn't spot any strings. No sleight of hand. Could the wood actually be growing in front of his eyes? He felt a lump in his throat. He swallowed hard, afraid that everybody could see the fear he was feeling. The wooden object now filled the gap between Aaron and Dudimose entirely. He forced a smile. He needed to maintain the impression that he was unfazed. But inside he was panicking. It didn't stop. The solid wood bent to accommodate the extra length. The slight curve he noticed, a soft arc to one side, swiftly became more pronounced. Another appeared on the other side to balance the first. The wood warped and bent alternately – this way, that way – concertinaing

45

across the floor. Dudimose's horrified intrigue focused his narrowed eyes exclusively on the wooden creature developing at his feet. They were tricking him in some way! He stamped his foot. Solid wood couldn't flex and pleat like fabric! Dudimose felt furious; indignant. In a burst of anger, he kicked out at the part closest to him. His foot struck the elliptical head but the solid thwack he anticipated never came. Instead, the substance squished softly around his sandalled toe and recoiled from the blow as if it were alive. His eyes widened. He pulled his foot, now strangely cold, away. Dudimose became aware of his breathing; slow and deep. He was on edge – afraid – and he didn't know exactly why. Something about this whole scenario wasn't right. He was used to the magic arts, but this felt different somehow. He was uncomfortable; considering leaving. No! That would appear like weakness. He was Pharaoh. He had to face this strangeness. And win.

Dudimose inhaled deeply to prepare himself and looked up to meet the gaze of Aaron, and Moses who he suspected was the real mastermind behind this. He opened his mouth to speak, but stopped before he began. The huge serpentine staff was moving. Dudimose tensed. It rose off the ground. Slowly, smoothly, it lifted into the air. The swirls behind unwound to allow it more freedom, causing it to sway slightly from side to side. Dudimose felt his stomach knot up. This piece of wood had become truly snake-like. If it weren't for the still visible wood grain on the surface, it would be almost indistinguishable. How were they doing this? It continued to rise. It was standing at half Pharaoh's height and still growing. Another coil opened out. One third of the huge creation was now elevated off the ground. The head was level with Dudimose's heart. He felt uneasy – sick – but he stood rigid on the spot. The slit, as if hinged, opened downwards and two curved white fangs slipped down from the flat upper surface. They were sharp and glistened with venom. Dudimose took a step back. Pink, fleshy tissue emerged in the triangle of the lower mouth and a tiny, forked, black ribbon flickered out. The wooden surface of the head grew two glassy green eyes and an unseen hand etched thin vertical black slits through their centres. Scales appeared. The first few seemed to emerge slowly from the wood: then they came in a strange chain reaction, faster and faster. They rippled rapidly down the snake's neck and along its length, following the coils and curves to the tip of the tail. Most were murky brown. Some were a distinct white, zigzagging their way along each side of the body. And the whole underside stretched into taut, dry, yellowish skin, marked with thin black lines. Dudimose gasped. He was face to face with a gargantuan King Cobra. It was the exact replica of the two which intertwined to form the golden crown of

Pharaohs – *his* symbol of power. But alive: living, breathing, moving and enormous. The snake enlarged its neck ribs to form a hood that began behind its eyes and extended down its neck to just beneath its open lower jaw. Dudimose was sweating, shivering. He recognised the pose. The cobra had made itself as large and imposing as possible. It felt threatened. It was ready to attack. Dudimose froze, but his heart pounded loudly inside his chest. He could hear his blood rushing through his ears.

Was this it? Had Moses and Aaron come to end his life?

Chapter 8:

Power games

This particular challenge felt personal. Just when he had sworn to achieve complete dominion over this festering disease of a nation, and in spite of the measures he'd taken to show them their requests were unwelcome, they had the audacity... they dared to come back here and use his own best weapon against him. They would not shake him so easily. He was King of Egypt. The serpent was *his* to control; it symbolised both his protection and his weapon. It had no power *against* him. He would simply not allow it. They needed to be shown how strong a Pharaoh could be.

He nodded his assent. Each of his sorcerers stood forward, preparing with enormous pride to perform their arts. His own sense of expectation raised his spirits. His sorcerers were good. They were the best. He had absolute faith that they would not fail him in this task.

The first was an older Egyptian with a lined forehead. He stepped forward, straining to straighten the natural slump in his back, raised his head and fixed his narrow, age-dimmed eyes on those of Moses and Aaron. With gnarled hands he held out a lidded basket made from reeds and, trembling slightly, removed the lid. In it sat a simple carving of a serpent. Its tail twisted and turned in convincing curves and great attention had been paid to the detail of the head. Its eyes were heavily polished so that they appeared glassy. The hood was open. Its head inclined naturally forward and it had the strange appearance of movement even before the craftsman took hold of it. It was a charm; an extra layer of protection for Dudimose. If the amulet round his neck failed to protect the King of Egypt, this carving certainly would not. The old man presented it to Pharaoh with a bow and with a horrified glance at the real serpent, staggered back.

Moving together, the three younger Egyptians slowly stepped forward. Each held their right arm forward. Large squares of cloth covered the serpents Dudimose knew they were holding. The fabric hung down in folds over the tall, narrow shapes. He loved knowing the secret. He enjoyed the moment of superiority it gave him over the observers. He smirked. The sorcerers each took one of the corners between thumb and forefinger and whisked it off with a dramatic flourish. Dudimose smiled. He approved of the theatrical beginning. He noted their white knuckles and the tight grip they were keeping. He trusted these men implicitly. Each held the neck of a King Cobra; real creatures, kept and trained by his sorcerers. It was *his* symbol and he wasn't prepared to relinquish it to snivelling Israelites. The sorcerers ceremoniously tilted and turned the creatures this way and that to demonstrate their solid state. Finally, each kissed their serpent delicately on the top of its head. From his vantage point at the rear, Dudimose was witness to the constant grip the sorcerers maintained on the necks of the snakes. He knew that this was crucial to the success of the illusion. He'd once interrogated the charmers after a performance, unable to bear the element of mystery and determined that no man should know more than himself in any detail of Egyptian life. *He*, after all, must maintain control over all things. As a result, he knew now that the sorcerers were exerting exactly the right amount of pressure on one particular nerve, causing the snakes to stiffen involuntarily. He knew too, that once released, the creatures would spring back to life, aggressively reacting to this treatment. Dudimose now, more than ever, was glad of this knowledge. This was exactly the sort of situation where proper preparation equipped him to maintain cool superiority and control. He hated surprises.

Dudimose nodded to the magicians again. They did not react immediately. They stood motionless. Waiting. Ensuring the undivided focus was theirs before flinging the snakes forcefully across the room. Dudimose smirked as Moses jumped. The three snakes hissed and drew themselves up, indignant at being cast so callously onto the cold marble floor. Dudimose allowed the corners of his mouth to turn up slightly and raised one superior eyebrow in the direction of Moses. He didn't speak. He didn't deem it necessary. He considered his point well made. Dudimose continued to beam with superior satisfaction. He had, after all, produced three snakes - beautiful specimens with vivid colouring, albeit only half the size of Aaron's one.

Dudimose now felt that enough time had been wasted on this competitive power game. He was about to dismiss the Israelites when Aaron's serpent stopped slithering and seemed to notice the others for the first time. It rose up once more, towering above the three and flicked its tongue threateningly. One snake lunged forward in an intrepid attempt to bite, but the monster arched backwards, its yellow underside stretched into a menacing curve. Before its attacker could reposition itself for a second attempt, Aaron's serpent swiftly stretched its lower jaw far beyond its usual extent. Using the pliable skin around its face to allow this incredible manoeuvre, its mouth doubled in size. With a smooth, sinister swoop, it engulfed the head of the smaller snake. Now it used its teeth to grip the prey in position. Red fluid spurted out of the pierced skin and ran erratically down the scales. The long, bloodied tail hung out one side of its mouth and flailed around hopelessly. Dudimose looked sideways at his sorcerers. He had seen one snake eat another before. It was a common occurrence. But not like this. Dudimose was entirely unprepared for what he saw. And it unnerved him. Aaron's cobra simply swallowed. It seemed to suck the smaller creature into itself. A loud slurp filled his ears as the tail slid smoothly into the fleshy mouth of the monster. It disappeared from sight in seconds and left no visible bulge in the snake's body. Dudimose blinked hard to dislodge the image. He felt a queasy knot in his stomach. That had been too easy. What was this creature?

An unexpected smile spread over Dudimose's face. The danger had passed. He was safe! The snake was now sated. It would find somewhere safe to lie dormant and digest its meal and wouldn't strike again for months. Moses' plan had backfired. Dudimose had lost one snake, but the sacrifice of one cobra was nothing to protect the life of a Pharaoh. He'd gladly give much more for that cause if it ever became necessary. He breathed an audible sigh of relief and his muscles relaxed. He would not die today. He was back in control: Exactly where he liked to be. He opened his eyes. Right…

A high-pitched defensive hiss brought him out of his trance. It had struck again! Ibiya grabbed his arm. His fingers dug in to Dudimose's flesh. The second cobra was attempting to ward off the attack. It dodged and swayed, hissing and spitting venom at the larger creature. It was feisty. It would not surrender without a good fight. But it couldn't really compete. Aaron's serpent struck fast and clean. Its fangs pierced the skin in one deft movement. Blood spurted out in arcs. Ibiya's grip on Dudimose tightened. The giant held its grip as its prey writhed and struggled, hissing and flicking its tongue. It writhed left and right, absorbing the violent resistance of its prey in smooth swaying waves. Dudimose watched intently until the body of the smaller cobra went limp. Its head flopped and Aaron's serpent finally released it. Blood dripped from its fangs. Dudimose pulled his arm free of his son's grip. The third snake seemed to know it would be hopeless to fight. It was slithering slowly back towards the sorcerers. Fleeing. The rhythmic sway of its curves made it seem graceful in defeat as it tried to appease the larger creature. But the huge king cobra stretched open its gaping jaws again. It would not be bought off so easily. It bowed its head to the ground and scooped up the tail of the retreating coward. At the same time, it caught the head of its limp victim. It closed its mouth around its meal and rose up from the ground. Its glassy green eyes glistened defiantly. From one corner of its mouth hung a limp, lifeless tail, and from the other, a head; eyes still alert, tongue still flickering. Venom dribbled in winding paths down the snake's scales and dripped onto Dudimose's floor. The droplets seeped into a puddle of blood and swirled through it like marble. The serpent flung its head round in one final violent motion, sending droplets of blood flying, showering Dudimose and Ibiya. It swallowed. The snakes were sucked back into the creature and were gone. Dudimose's sorcerers looked to him in horror. 'Leave,' he directed them and waited for them to go before addressing Moses. 'And you too. Take this monster out of my court.'

Aaron stooped down and gently held his serpent's tail. As he lifted it from the ground, a violent ripple travelled the entire length of its body. Aaron braced himself against the force. The head snapped into line with a jolt. Then it stiffened. Dudimose folded his arms. He raised an impatient eyebrow. *Get out. Just get out!* Every muscle in the serpent's body contracted at once until the snake appeared hard and inflexible as the marble beneath it. Its head shrunk back into itself, leaving the redundant skin hanging in large wrinkled folds. Dudimose sighed impatiently. The serpent's eyes were now empty of life; the tongue immobile and silent, the fangs hanging oddly from the vacant skin. The body slowly shortened. The scaly skin detached itself in one limp deposit and slid to the floor where it lay crumpled and hollow. Ibiya wrinkled up his nose and put a hand over his mouth. Aaron stood up, raised the staff to his side and turned to leave. Moses followed wordlessly.

'Come, Ibiya. We have work to do.'

Ibiya stood looking at the empty skin discarded on the marble. 'Father...'

'I want to talk to you about my building project.'

'Father, you could have died.'

'Their snake is powerless against me. I have my amulet, and the carved charm.'

'That was not an ordinary snake! It was a real wooden staff. They came here with no pretension, no show. Their God...'

'No, Ibiya. They have nothing we don't have. They can do nothing we can't also do. They came here to scare me and they have failed. I'm not threatened. They will not get what they want from me so easily. Now, my architect is meeting us tomorrow...'

'Yes, you produced snakes too. It's an illusion. You know that! But don't you think it's significant that their snake swallowed yours? Ominous?'

'No. No, I don't. Moses would have been educated in the ways of Egyptian sorcery amongst other things during his time in the palace. He probably spent his years away perfecting his art.'

'Their power clearly overwhelmed yours. It's a sign; a warning perhaps.'

'I'm still here, Ibiya. If they were that powerful, I wouldn't be. I won today. Their God has no power. None! Now come; you criticise my architectural plans and yet you have not produced any of your own. I need to see evidence if I am to believe your ideas can work.'

Chapter 9:

Rasui

Rasui stumbled through the door of his overcrowded house, drained and exhausted. Everyone was there. This was the last thing he needed at the end of his indescribably frightening day; the whole family waiting to hear how it had gone. But if he'd expected anything other than this welcome, he'd been deluding himself. Rasui was the eldest of the many uneducated brothers and sisters and the first to find work. His father was unbearably proud of him. The gushing adoration made Rasui uncomfortable. His mother was no better. She was anxious about the treatment he would receive as the youngest of the lowest ranking servants in the Palace of the Pharaoh. Her constant fretting irritated him. He scanned the expectant faces. Even his smallest brother, barely walking, seemed to be waiting for him to say something. Rasui looked at his feet, shuffled into the room and squeezed himself into a space in the corner.

His parents looked at each other. His mother opened her mouth to launch into her inquisition, but his father silenced her with a look. He shrugged and shook his head slightly. She dutifully closed her mouth but continued to watch her son, a concerned wrinkle hovering on her brow. Rasui's closest sister was not so tactful.

'Well?' she demanded. 'How was it? What did they make you do? Did you get to see him? Probably not. Not on your first day. They probably had you…'

'Leave it,' Rasui muttered. With a sullen frown, he looked sideways at her. The others were still watching every movement for any clue that would tell them what was going on inside Rasui's head.

'What? Aren't you going to tell us all about it? That's so unfair! We've been waiting all day.' She glared at him. 'Rasui! Why not? Are you in trouble already?'

'Kepi, that's enough!' Her father was stern. 'Your brother has had a long day. Let's all let him be. Yes?' He looked around the room, waiting until each nod of agreement was given. Kepi held out as long as she could, but her father's well-practised piercing glare was eventually too much for even her stubborn determination.

'Alright,' she huffed. But I'm going to find out. She pulled herself to her feet and headed for the door. 'Someone will know.'

Rasui sighed. He loved all his siblings – even Kepi – but at times the longing for a little privacy threatened to overwhelm him. He sat quietly with his head down until the others had given up watching him and returned to their usual bustle, then snuck out to the roof. He was hungry, but he was more than prepared to forego family mealtime to avoid reliving his day.

Settling down on his back, Rasui stretched out his aching legs. He breathed in deep lungfuls of wonderful evening air and watched the light fade. Gradually the tension in his shoulders disappeared and his mind cleared of all its crazy thoughts. It's only a job, he reminded himself. And that's probably not the strangest thing I'll see in my time. His head began to lilt to one side and his eyelids flickered. With a yawn and a stretch, Rasui welcomed sleep.

But the serpent's face returned almost instantly – larger and uglier than before. The green eyes burned, the scales glistened wet with slime that hung in stringy strands and dripped ominously onto the ground. Two white fangs protruded from its open mouth, large, sharp and dangerous. The black sliver of a tongue flicked out at Rasui. He leapt up. Rubbed his face. Blinked. The image was still there. He was awake, wasn't he? Yes, yes he was. Why was that monster still here? It'd been a dream. It must have… Flame-like flickers danced around in the serpent's eyes. Venom ran down its fangs. The serpent moved toward his pallid face, its ribbed hood curving round him, about to engulf him; he focused on the fleshy pink inside of its mouth, growing larger and wider and…

Rasui screamed. Kepi screamed.

'Its me! Rasui, It's me. Kepi!' She shook his shoulders.

Rasui blinked and pulled back. The glassy green faded to reveal the warm concern worn in his sister's dark brown eyes. Her arms surrounded him where the serpent's hood had loomed moments earlier.

'Kepi.'

'Rasui, are you alright?'

'I don't know. It... I don't...' Rasui turned away. Kepi and the serpent were still intermingled in his confusion and he couldn't look at her. A bad dream was one thing. But he'd been awake, unable to shake the dream off - to distinguish it from reality. His heart was still racing. He sank to the ground, his hands shaking, and stared at the palace. He knew that tomorrow he'd have to go back.

Chapter 10:

One

'Ibiya, I don't disagree in principle, but you are not backing up your observations with any sensible alternatives.'

'I...'

'We are meeting with my architect *today*, Ibiya. Your sketch has no measurements, no...'

'I will have a proper design, Dad. I have so many ideas, it's just... There's been a lot happening and...'

The newly risen sun was beating down on Dudimose and his heir as they took their usual morning stroll to the Nile. The daily walk and talk was becoming a valuable time for them to discuss matters openly, away from the listening ears at the palace and the constraints of expectation and duty that existed there. During this time, Ibiya could be honest about his thoughts and Dudimose could lean more towards being parent and friend than tutor and critic. It was proving beneficial for the whole mentoring relationship.

'I know, Ibiya. But there's always a lot happening. There always will be. I need to see a much better design before that meeting. Otherwise, I'm afraid I will be continuing with my original plan.'

'Dad, I... could you give me a few more days?'

'There may be something in what you say about needing more originality, but I need to see what it will actually look like. I need to know how it will fit into its surroundings. I need to know how to resource the project. I need... This temple is supposed to be my masterpiece and I will not compromise that. But I am giving you your chance. Give me something substantial to work with. Produce proper plans for me today.'

Ibiya did not respond. His attention had been distracted. His already solemn face quickly drained of all colour. Dudimose looked around to see what had caused this reaction in his son. Moses and Aaron were back. Dudimose felt his jaw tighten. He drew himself up with more composure than he felt. His eyes were drawn to the staff Moses held in his hand. He had not forgotten the snake. He still felt livid when he thought about it. His head was flooded with angry thoughts. Outwardly, he remained serene.

Moses began to speak. 'The Lord, the God of the Hebrews, sent me to you, saying "Let my people go, that they may serve me in the wilderness." But behold, you have not listened until now.'

Dudimose summoned every ounce of strength to prevent his eyes rolling in frustration. This again! He thought he'd made himself clear. His Israelite slaves were needed here. They would remain under *his* control, to serve his purposes. They had not yet produced enough bricks for the plan he was making. When the temple project began, he would need the manpower only these slaves could provide. This 'Lord' had no rights in *his* territory. And no power that Dudimose had not matched. He produced a cobra. Dudimose produced three. He did not need to listen to this. He strode past Moses to the bank of the Nile and kicked off his sandals. Perhaps Moses would realise he was unwelcome if he received no response.

The cool water lapped refreshingly around Dudimose's ankles. He held out his arms to steady himself as he carefully stepped down the slope. He felt his way with his bare feet to the familiar ledge where he liked to stand knee-deep, watching the ripples he'd created travel across the width of the river, noticing the fascinating intersections as they rebounded off the opposite bank. Today he didn't bother. He couldn't enjoy it. Moses had intruded on his time, invading his space so he couldn't relax properly. Dudimose hated to be observed when he wasn't in official Pharaoh-mode. He scowled. His pride took over. He bent his knees, lowering himself into the water until he was submerged to his waist.

Moses was undeterred by being ignored.

'Thus says the Lord, "By this you shall know that I am the Lord: behold, I will strike the water that is in the Nile with the staff that is in my hand, and it will be...'

Dudimose held his nose and plunged down into the Nile. For a few glorious moments he couldn't hear anything except the rushing of water past his ears. Moses' voice had been drowned out along with everything except his own thoughts. It was blissful. Tiny bubbles escaped from his nose and drifted up past his eyes like a sand clock, counting down the time he had left to enjoy his escapism. He closed them and smiled to himself.

When he couldn't hold his breath any longer, Dudimose kicked back up and emerged from the surface, shaking water from his head. It ran down his neck and over his face. The cool water refreshed his body and arms as it flowed across his skin. He filled his lungs with fresh air opened his eyes. Moses was still there. Dudimose's mind went wild. It was racing. *Is this a deliberate insult? What is he still doing here? This is* my *Nile. And at this time of day, the Nile is reserved for* my *use. Nobody comes near. How did he get so close in the first place? Where were the guards? Who has allowed this...?* Ibiya remained on the bank.

'The fish that are in the Nile will die, and the Nile will become foul, and the Egyptians will find difficulty in drinking water from the Nile.'

Dudimose plunged his hands in and watched the ripples spread slowly outward. *What was Moses talking about? Difficulty in drinking from the Nile? Nonsense!* He cupped his hands and drew them slowly up. Water spilled over his thumbs and down his wrists. He raised them to his lips and took a long refreshing slurp. He filled his cheeks, enjoying the cooling sensation and then swallowed. A dribble trickled down his chin and neck. There's nothing wrong with this water. From the corner of his eye, Dudimose watched Moses and Aaron. They were talking. Deciding to leave, he hoped. Ibiya looked pale. He was beckoning. He was probably too embarrassed to bathe in front of strangers, Dudimose thought. He probably thinks I shouldn't either. He decided not to pressure Ibiya to come in, but he wasn't ready to get out yet either. Dudimose pulled his cupped hands from the gentle flow of the Nile again and splashed water onto his face. He exhaled as cool trickles ran over his features and dripped onto his torso. This was perfect. He saw Aaron hold his staff out over the water. *What was he doing?* He scooped a second handful of water onto his face. Aaron struck the water forcefully with the base of the staff. Dudimose slapped the surface in retaliation. The shockwaves reached the ledge and lapped at his knees. They were interrupting his leisure time. He dove into the Nile again. These people were hanging around like a foul smell and they didn't deserve to see his face. Violent ripples spread from the base of Aaron's staff and travelled across the entire width of the Nile. Dudimose could feel the waves above his head as he swam, pulling himself through the water with strong strokes. Swift folds, like windswept sand around Dudimose's pyramid, softened gradually into undulating dunes as they glided outwards in their perfectly formed circle. To begin with they were clear as the heavens. But every new ripple was slightly less transparent and a touch darker in colour. Ibiya's eyes were wide. There was a smooth and strangely captivating transition through translucent pink to deep ruby red, and then the colour darkened.

Dudimose reached the opposite bank and performed a perfect turn. He righted himself for the return. But a strange sensation was gradually seeping over him as he kicked beneath the surface. The water didn't feel cool any more as it flowed over his skin. It became tepid. He wouldn't have noticed that in itself, but it was getting darker too – much darker. A spiralling ruby streak had passed in front of him - he'd hardly had time to focus on it before everything had gone black. *What had Moses released? Was it another serpent? Where was it now?* His senses were heightened. He was on edge. He became aware of the temperature gradually continuing to rise. There was a strange taste on his lips that hadn't been there before and he felt his heartbeat race. *What was happening?* He needed to get out of this water. He desperately held onto his breath, concentrating on strong, smooth movements. Inexplicable warmth quickly enveloped him. He built up the rhythmic swing, pulling his arms faster, kicking harder. He was determined to free himself from this strangeness before it got any worse. He couldn't tell how far he had left to go. The darkness was impenetrable now. He couldn't see his own arms moving in front of his face. The taste on his lips grew stronger. It was odd – metallic. His head felt faint. He was dizzy. He pushed short spurts of air out through his nose to dislodge the overpowering smell that had gripped him. He needed to breathe fresh air. There was none left in his mouth. Dudimose raised his head and flung his arms downwards to propel himself up. As his hands touched his sides, his skin felt slimy. In reflex, he pulled them away, swirling round and gasping before his head broke the surface. Thick, sticky liquid poured into his mouth. He gagged. He writhed. The substance got up his nose. A pain seared through his head. He panicked. He swallowed. Dudimose's legs were flailing. His arms flung wide. His head convulsed, twisting and shaking, sending shudders through his body. He emerged from the Nile gagging, spluttering and heaving. There was screaming. He coughed. He spat. The odour was making him feel sick. He swayed dizzily, struggling to keep himself upright. The taste permeated his mouth and burned his throat. He cast around for Ibiya, but everything was a blur. Red streaks had been smeared across his eyeballs so everything around him appeared to be slathered with crimson. He squinted to focus and recoiled in pain. His eyes stung. They burned. He yelled out. His strong anguished cry mingled with his son's incessant screams. He rubbed hard with his fists, but made it worse. The pain was blinding. Blinking was unbearable. Tears streamed from his eyes, down his face and into the corners of his mouth. The salty liquid mingled with the slimy, metallic tasting substance that he hadn't been able to shift and his stomach lurched. Vomit raced into the back of his mouth, but slid down his throat again. It was vile. He swilled saliva round his mouth and spat another huge globule into the Nile, but still could not get rid of the foul tasting substance.

'Ibiya!'

Dudimose was disorientated and confused. *What was happening?* He swirled around, trying to catch sight of Ibiya. He moved his hands to rub his eyes again but stopped himself just in time. He blinked furiously, wincing in agony, but intent on clearing his vision. Ibiya's frenzied screaming stopped. Everything was quiet; eerily still and silent. Dudimose wiped one slimy hand over his head.

Gradually his vision cleared. He saw Ibiya, sobbing, eyes wide in fear. He saw the bank where his sandals lay abandoned by a boulder. He looked down and saw brilliant red channels of water flowing along the course of the Nile. He lifted his hands to see trails of red running down his fingers and across his palms. Blood was trickling over his wrists, down his arms and from his head down the small of his neck. His white robe was saturated. A hot wave swept through Dudimose's body and his temples throbbed. He narrowed his eyes, glared with all his might and emitted a long, loud, angry yowl.

Chapter 11:

Problems

Aaron lifted the staff. Thick beads of blood clung to its base and dripped heavily off into the now burgundy river with an eerie plop. He gave it a shake, sending a spray of tiny red balls scattering in all directions. Without a word, he and Moses walked away in the direction of the palace.

Dudimose stared after them incredulously. Thick, syrupy liquid was travelling slowly down his back and arms. Around his neck and in the creases of his elbows and knees, blood was starting to coagulate. It felt sticky. Dudimose felt dirty; contaminated. He looked down at his blood-soaked robes. The fine Egyptian linen was heavy and clung uncomfortably to his skin. He tore the fabric band from his shoulder in disgust and allowed it to hang down from his waist. He couldn't look less like a Pharaoh if he tried and the insult stung his pride. He turned on Ibiya.

'Where are they going? Look what they've done to me, Ibiya!'

His son waited a moment before replying as gently as he could. 'They did warn you…'

The words struck Dudimose at his core. His jaw dropped. Did his own son, his firstborn just say...? It sounded too much like a challenge. His anger exploded. He aimed it at the only person left with him.

'Are you saying this is my fault?'

'No, dad. I just... think it wasn't really a surprise. You saw him standing there with the staff. You must have known something...'

'But blood! Blood in my beautiful river?'

'Perhaps it's not as random as you think. The snake was an attack on your revered symbol, the blood...'

'What! What possible reason could there be for this filth?' *Was Ibiya defending them?* Dudimose's misdirected anger strengthened, making Ibiya almost afraid to speak the words. Dudimose looked insistent. He would receive an answer, whether or not he liked what he heard. He saw Ibiya struggle, knowing he had no choice. When he spoke, it was as softly as he could muster.

'Perhaps it's a kind of judgement – he is *their* god – for the Hebrew babies. All those boys...'

'Perhaps.' Dudimose was tight-lipped. His tone made it clear that he did not agree and Ibiya stopped without pressing his point. Dudimose nodded, pleased that his son had recognised it would have been foolish to continue. 'Where are they going now?'

'Um... The lake? They'll be looking for more water.'

Dudimose smiled. 'I must change out of this spoiled robe and I have several urgent matters to attend to before I...'

'What urgent matters? Should I accompany you?'

'No, son. You misunderstand. I simply intend to make Moses and Aaron wait – a very long time. They must learn not to irritate me and the guards will hold them until my arrival.'

Ibiya opened his mouth to respond. Then he hesitated.

'What is it, Ibiya? I've already explained to you why these people must wait. After this insult, you must see why I must always keep the upper hand.' He scratched his arm. The blood was beginning to dry out, pulling on the fine hairs of his skin. He could feel it tightening all over his body. His skin was taut, stretched and felt as though somebody was twisting it. He rolled his muscles around and felt the dried blood crack.

'It's not that. It's just... the guards... I don't think they... it's that staff. Ever since the serpent there have been so many rumours... everyone knows. They're scared of it. Moses gained access to the Nile. That shouldn't be possible. Why not the lake, or the palace?'

Without a response, Dudimose turned and stormed after the representatives of this Israelite 'Lord'. They were beginning to make him look foolish and he would not stand for that.

Dudimose rounded the corner of the palace. He had covered the distance from the river faster than ever before and he was sweating. This is not how a Pharaoh behaves. He felt on edge and a little out of control. He talked to himself as he paced along the outer colonnade. Calm down. Slow. Serene. Sovereign. He swept under the archway and stopped dead. His last footstep echoed from the columns around him like a cracking whip. He stared. *No. This was not possible.* Wine-coloured liquid filled the ceremonial lake. *Where are they?* He looked but there was nobody there. They had already gone. He slowly approached the edge. The foul stink filled his nostrils again. His stomach churned and he retched. He couldn't stop himself. He clutched his abdomen as he vomited into the vile, polluting substance. He crouched, panting. The stench of the vomit combined with a distinct odour of sun-scorched blood made his head spin. Dudimose steadied himself and slowly straightened up. He spoke aloud to himself.

'You are Pharaoh: *King* of Egypt. This is *your* lake, *your* Nile. This does not happen without your permission. It stops NOW!'

He entered the palace issuing clear, concise instructions to the nearest messenger and went to his quarters to change. As clean as he could achieve without fresh water, and clothed in crisp spotless linen, he felt back in control. When he entered the court, it was with his head high and his composure intact. Ibiya joined him, throwing a questioning look in his direction. Dudimose did not respond. As far as Ibiya was aware, he did not even notice. He was aloof and commanding again.

With a nod, he summoned his sorcerers. The elderly man, who had provided the carved snake charm, tottered across the marble floor and presented a scroll of papyrus. He cleared his throat and in his shaky tone read precise instructions for the art of turning water blood-red. Dudimose thanked him.

'Pharaoh, I'm sorry to interrupt.' The messenger bowed. 'I bring a communication.' Dudimose gave him a brief nod to continue. 'The catch basins and dykes are filled with a thick red liquid resembling blood. The farmers are concerned that they will be unable to irrigate the crops properly.'

'I am aware of the situation regarding our water supply. It is under control. Instruct the farm workers not to open the dykes to water the fields until I permit them to do so. Instruct them to make extra visits to the temple during this period to appease the gods. You may leave.' As he did so, another two messengers scrambled into the court, bowing low.

'Pharaoh, may I...' Dudimose nodded without waiting to hear the request in full. 'I have come from the temple. Many lay priests are reporting problems with the water for washing the statues. They are afraid because it has turned red. They fear the gods are angered and they will be punished. Also...' at this point, the messenger hesitated. He exhaled slowly to prepare himself. 'Also, they are unwilling to take the prescribed cold baths as the water is... foul.' He bit his lower lip.

'If I may,' interrupted the next, 'I have come from the Nile-view residences. The nobles complain that their children are unable to swim, their drinking water is contaminated and that their spear fishing has had to be abandoned as the fish are found to be floating. That is to say, they are all dead.'

'Is that all?'

'Almost, Pharaoh, except to say that the nobility also complain of their streets being overrun by peasants, digging around the banks of the Nile in search of fresh water. They have asked them to leave, but the peasants are rebelling. And that they object to the smell emanating from the Nile.'

'As I have recently informed the farming community, I am aware of the issues regarding the water supply in Egypt at present. I will be rectifying this at the earliest opportunity. In the meantime, please instruct both the priests and the nobility to remain calm. There is nothing to worry about.'

Ibiya turned to his father.

'Don't speak, Ibiya. Moses would love me to be concerned. He wants to create panic in Egypt. I will not give him that satisfaction. Watch this.'

The remaining sorcerers stepped forward. Each had acquired a small wooden bowl of clear water. Dudimose assumed those peasants, digging around for spring water, had provided this. It couldn't really be that hard to acquire then. Simultaneously they began their incantations. All three were chanting strange words in mystical tones. It lacked harmony. The sounds clashed and assaulted Dudimose's ears. He hoped it would not last long. Each held a hand over their bowl and wafted it around in slow circles. He looked from the bowls to the faces of the magicians, furrowed in concentration. They were focused, solemn and convincing. When he looked back, the clear water had taken on a rusty orange-red hue.

'There,' said Dudimose. He clapped his hands together twice. 'They still have no power that I do not. None.' He strode straight across the court; the sorcerers scuttled apart to allow him through. As he passed them, he heard Ibiya muttering 'might have been more helpful to turn the river back though.' Dudimose baulked. He looked like he had when he'd tasted a mouthful of Nile blood earlier that morning, but decided not to react. He'd talk with his son later, when they'd both calmed down. As he stormed towards the far side of the court, he almost collided with the messenger hurrying in.

'What is it?' he barked.

The messenger bowed his head. 'Pharaoh, the task masters over the Israelite slaves are furious. They say the Israelite supervisors are claiming they cannot work.'

'If they are complaining of thirst, I will implement an increase in their labour immediately. We will not have any more excuses for laziness.'

'No, Pharaoh. That is not the reason.'

'Then what? What could possibly be the problem?'

'"Blood" does not work. Without water, they are unable to make clay for the bricks.'

Chapter 12:

Umayma

Umayma lifted her baby sister down from her hip and handed her her special doll from the table. It was made from a single piece of leftover linen, folded and knotted to resemble a small person. It was dirty and worn especially on top of its head where she loved to rub it against her cheek, but that didn't matter. It would keep Sagira occupied and Umayma needed that now. It wouldn't be long before her mother returned from the grinding stones, hungry and tired. It was her responsibility to prepare a meal, and to make sure both her sisters were fed and ready for sleep.

For the past week or two, Umayma's father had been under extra pressure at work because of the problems with the water. He would remain in the fields until late again today. Even now that the Nile flowed clear again, the crops were dangerously wilted and some animals quite seriously ill. The issues it had caused could take weeks to resolve. If the plants in the fields didn't recover it could still be affecting food supplies this time next year. Umayma was just glad to be able to cook again though. The week without water had been horrible for everyone. There'd been no bread or beer or fish. They'd all survived on dried fruits, but that supply was now running low and this year's fruit wasn't nearly ready to be gathered yet. Umayma reached up for a large bowl from the shelf and took a scoopful of ground wheat from the jar. She added fig to flavour it.

'Umayma, I'm hungry,' Pili complained, coming in from the street and rolling a leather ball across the floor. Umayma heard giggles as the doll was dropped and baby Sagira pulled and shuffled her way across the floor after the ball.

'Can you bring me the water? I'm just making the bread now.'

'Will there be fish today?' Pili asked, spinning a small pottery top across the table.

'No. You know there are no fish left'

'Just bread?'

'And fruit.' The spinning top reached the edge of the table and tottered. Pili sighed and scooped up the top before stepping over Sagira to fetch the jug of water from the corner. She bent down to lift it and squealed.

'What is it?' Umayma asked.

'A frog. Behind the jug. It's staring at me.'

'Just bring the jug. It'll soon go.'

The frog hopped around the floor as Umayma kneaded the dough for the bread. Pili tried unsuccessfully to guide it toward the door. Its erratic hopping made it impossible to direct and it seemed to want to go anywhere but out. Sagira stroked her cheek with the doll's head for comfort and watched the process with a slightly bemused expression.

'Umayma!'

'What is it? I'm...' She looked up to see another three frogs coming in through the door. 'This is ridiculous. Where are they coming from?' She suspected one of Pili's friends was playing a joke. Umayma walked over to the door and peered out. There was nobody there. She sighed. They must have already run off to hide. She was about to return to her work when something caught her eye. Shock froze her face. Hundreds of frogs were hopping along the street away from the river. The dusty ground was spattered with blobs of smooth, brilliant green. They leapt unpredictably, following one another in sudden waves of erratic movement along the street. Children were grabbing their toys and running indoors. People were peering from windows and doorways, baffled by the odd sight. Several more frogs jumped into the house past Umayma's legs. Sagira had started to cry. She turned and swept her up, dislodging the offending frog from her baby sister's lap. It made a leap for the table. Umayma jiggled Sagira up and down on her hip to calm her and grabbed the bowl from the table.

'We need to block the doorway. Help me tip this table,' she instructed Pili, depositing the bowl on the floor. There was no response. Her sister stared wide-eyed at the small green creatures with their oddly protruding eyes and splayed feet – skin stretched thinly between each toe. They were out of place here, and unwelcome.

'Quickly, before any more come in.'

Pili grabbed one end of the table and tipped. Umayma held tightly to Sagira as she crouched to lower her end to the floor. Then they shoved and pushed the table, leaning hard against it until it covered the opening. Umayma handed Sagira to Pili and crept slowly after a frog that had settled in the corner of the room. If she was careful, she could get rid of them all before her parents returned. She crouched down and slowly stalked towards it. It looked at her goggle-eyed and croaked. Its throat puffed out to three times its usual size and the strange sound made baby Sagira cry again. Umayma looked round and the frog took its opportunity to dart away. She sighed. This wasn't going to be easy.

'Umayma, look.' Pili pointed to the bowl of dough they'd abandoned on the floor. A frog sat on the squashy surface, flicking its long, thin tongue.

'No!' She grabbed the bowl, holding it at arm's length as she scurried across the room and lowered it over the upturned table. She tipped the dough-filled bowl gently until the frog hopped off into the street. It hopped twice more and then without warning extended its powerful legs fully, springing up onto the window ledge. Umayma was horrified. She had no idea they could jump so high. Now what?

Chapter 13:

Two

Dudimose hesitated before entering the court. Inside, Moses and Aaron were waiting. They had come to the palace at *his* request. He was finding the situation very uncomfortable and for a moment he considered the possibility that he was about to do the wrong thing. This whole situation had been a public relations disaster; his popularity in Egypt was being compromised. Would this make him seem weaker? *No.* He must not allow himself to think that way. This is what the public would want him to do. He had a responsibility to end the chaos – even if that meant humbling himself and asking for help.

But it went against every instinct of his nature. He backed away from the entrance. It wasn't done yet. He could still change his mind. The thought of going in there and giving them what they'd wanted all along made his heart ache. It was not right. It would be giving in to their pressure tactics. He would be backing down. He kicked the floor in frustration. There must be another solution. *Think.*

But there wasn't. He'd agonised over it all night. After all, he hadn't been able to sleep because of the amphibians crawling around all over his bed, croaking at him constantly. Their smooth, wet skin and webbed feet had made him feel a little creepy. He remembered shuddering as he looked at them. He'd felt as though their strange protruding eyes were constantly watching him. Huge groups of them huddled together, mocking him in deep croaks with their throats puffing, swelling in and out, and their mouths closed. He'd paced the room, planning his route back to normality and order, while they had hopped around chaotically, doing nothing to calm his mind. Their powerful hind legs propelled their tiny bodies huge distances across the room. More than once, he'd jumped, startled as one landed at his feet or collided with his legs. Their long, thin, sticky tongues appeared and disappeared at incredible speeds when they detected a fly or spider. He'd been permanently on edge. What had he done to deserve this? What could possibly have angered the gods so much? He needed their support now and they were not providing it. That did not bode well. He needed to gain their favour. He'd longed to gather up the frogs and remove them, but he hadn't dared touch these sacred creatures in case he upset the gods any more. He couldn't risk that. He made a mental note to speak to the priests at the earliest opportunity. Egypt was being subjected to irritating… inconvenient… humiliation by the god of *his slaves*! He'd always said they were getting above themselves and this just proved it. He wrung his hands as he regretted not taking any more drastic action against them sooner. He had to get them back under control. But first he had to deal with these frogs. Dudimose thought back to his conversation with Ibiya earlier that morning.

★ ★ ★

'If you were nicer to them – consistently nicer – and fair, surely they'd be more willing to cooperate.'

So naive, Bless him! 'Ibiya, you have no idea how dangerously ineffective that would be. It's a delusion. Sweet, but flawed.'

'But, dad. Just think about it...' His eyes implored Dudimose.

'It would play straight into their hands. They'd be bending every rule I gave them, until they got exactly what they wanted.'

'I'm not so sure.' Dudimose was not going to be convinced.

'No. You're wrong. And I have to overrule you on this. I'm sorry.'

★ ★ ★

But it had given Dudimose an idea. A somewhat more devious one, but he liked it so much more for that. And, more importantly, it was going to work. If he was 'nice' long enough to get Moses and Aaron to help him remove this frog issue, then... then he'd be back in control of Egypt and of the slaves; full, heavy-handed, authoritative control. His problems would be over. They would submit to him; to his power over them. He'd give them no choice. And in doing that, he would also teach Ibiya the correct way to handle such difficulties. It was the next stage of his training and, after that conversation, an urgent and vital one. So, now he just had to get on with the act. Acting repentant was not part of Dudimose's usual vocabulary – it wasn't a great skill of his. It wasn't something he'd really had cause to practise before now. Still, if duty necessitated it...

Dudimose trod cautiously, looking for clear patches of ground where he could place his feet. He tottered between the frogs, being careful not to harm any of the sacred creatures in any way. He faced Moses and Aaron. This was painful. He raised his voice over the perpetual chorus of croaking.

'Entreat the Lord that he may remove the frogs from me and from my people.' He scratched his face absent-mindedly, trying not to show the effort that had cost him. Aaron looked stunned. Moses furrowed his brow. He seemed confused. Neither said anything. Dudimose waited. He had hoped to avoid this next part, but there was still no response, so they left him with no choice. *They knew that, didn't they? This is what they were waiting for.* He hated to give them the satisfaction. 'And I will let the people go, that they may sacrifice to the Lord.' He emphasised the last part heavily. He still suspected their intention was not *only* to go for three days. It was important that they knew he was fully in control of the terms of this deal and that he expected *his* slaves to return. He'd make sure they did. Moses looked at Dudimose, trying to read his face. Pharaoh kept his features as neutral as possible. This was a game now, a little battle between them, and he was giving away nothing of his strategy. He watched as Moses weighed up how best to respond. When he did, it was with all the right words, feigning deference. But the insincerity could not have been plainer to Dudimose and it stung like a whip.

'The honour is yours to tell me: when shall I entreat for you *and* your servants *and* your people...'

Dudimose opened his mouth to answer but Moses had not finished.

'...that the frogs be destroyed from *you* and *your* houses...'

Moses was enjoying this. Dudimose felt his shoulders rise and tense up. He felt so insulted. Was it really necessary to remind him of the problem *they* had caused? Even now, the frog song accompanied this meeting. They were hopping around his feet. He had not forgotten! He could not forget. His eyes were narrowing, but he restrained his tongue. He deliberately forced his shoulders back down.

'...that they may only be left in the Nile.'

Let them enjoy the upper hand for now, Dudimose thought to himself. It won't last long.

'Tomorrow,' he replied. He didn't trust himself to say more than that single word without compromising the job he'd come to do. He wanted to stamp. He'd felt like saying NOW! But he couldn't afford to appear desperate.

'May it be according to your word, that you may know there is no one like the Lord our God.'

Yes there is! Dudimose seethed inside. *The 'Lord' your god has done nothing my sorcerers cannot. There's no guarantee he can even do this.* He remembered Ibiya's comment.

★ ★ ★

'Rather than showing you have power *equal* to the Israelite's god by replicating their tricks, you should demonstrate power *greater* than theirs by reversing them instead.'

Dudimose had been confused. What did he mean?

'Producing even more frogs may not have been the most helpful course of action.'

Dudimose loved his son. He needed to work on his sense of timing though. Why was he telling him this after the event?

★ ★ ★

He'd thought Ibiya's was a logical idea, but he had not quite dared to test it. After all, it would be extremely embarrassing if his sorcerers were not able to remove the frogs. It struck him now that it would be equally embarrassing for Moses if he was not able to either. Dudimose gained some satisfaction from that daydream, although it would leave him to deal with a rather tricky amphibian problem.

Lost in these thoughts, Dudimose had not dismissed his visitors. He looked up now to do so, but they only took this as a cue to elaborate further.

'The frogs will depart from you and your houses and your servants and your people; they will be left only in the Nile.'

He felt his hands balling up at his sides. He knew they were playing with him by going on about this. He would not react. He pressed his lips together. To Dudimose's great relief, they finally left the court. It had cost a great deal of restraint to go into that meeting and make a request of his own slaves. And they had toyed with him. Ibiya used to have a little wooden monkey with glass eyes and limbs that moved. He'd played with that thing for hours at a time, positioning it one way and then another, controlling its every move. Dudimose felt like that monkey and he did not like the experience. He reassured himself that once the frogs were gone, he would pay them back for every moment of their insolence. Three times over.

Chapter 14:

Knowing God

'Shh!' Dudimose silenced his son and held out an arm to stop him in his tracks. 'Don't say a word.'

Ibiya froze. Only his eyes continued to move. Wide and watchful, they darted left and right, scanning for any slight movement. It was an abrupt change. Moments before, father and son had been casually strolling together. The conversation had flowed easily. Now they stood not moving; alert, on edge and waiting.

'We missed it.' Dudimose finally broke the silence. 'What were you saying?' They relaxed and began to walk again. Ibiya shrugged. It couldn't have been important.

'I need to talk to you anyway.'

Ibiya took long, low awkward strides through the marsh. He placed his feet carefully and moved forward slowly, trying not to disturb the long grasses. Even so, they rustled noisily as they drifted back into position behind him. At his side, Dudimose seemed to glide effortlessly through the grass. In contrast to his son's deliberate, conscious motion, his was smooth and automatic. He had done this many times before.

'I do not want you to... inflate your opinion of yourself on account of what I am about to say, Ibiya,' He paused to gauge his son's reaction. 'But I'd like to hear your thoughts about the Moses' fiasco.'

'Dad, I...'

'Before you speak, you should know that I... do not in any way regret the manner in which I have handled... matters. In fact, I sincerely hope you have been taking notes. However, I want to... assess... your own position on the subject. Knowing what you have understood will help me to plan the next stages of your education.'

Ibiya was watching his father from the corner of his eye. Dudimose continued to walk beside him, making it difficult for his son to read his expression – deliberately so. In truth, Dudimose was beginning to doubt his approach a little. He was having trouble dislodging Ibiya's insight from his mind. It came so naturally and easily to his son. Was there anything in it? He hoped not. Dudimose's own practice was based on his years of experience. It had worked for him so far. He hoped that talking it through with Ibiya would help convince him that his son's comments were simply empty ideas – nothing more.

'Well, I'll start with an observation, Dad. Moses and Aaron kept to the deal. They prayed to their god at the agreed time.'

'That is true. But they were in a weak position. They knew they needed to impress me.'

'More importantly,' Ibiya continued without paying much attention to his father, 'their god responded at the appointed time.'

'Yes.'

'That shows control; total control. Not only can he inflict a curse like this over all your territory...' Dudimose winced. '...but he also has the power to stop it and to do that at a specified time. With due respect, I don't believe your sorcerers could have achieved that.'

'We will never know, Ibiya. I did not ask them to and as the frogs are no longer with us, sadly I can't. They were able to produce frogs...'

'Which made your problems worse!'

'...and they may well have been capable of getting rid of them... but, in any case, we are relieved...'

Dudimose's voice faded away to nothing as his eyes locked onto something in the distance. His arm flew out, index finger raised in warning. He required silence. He pointed.

'There; to your left, moving within the grass.'

'Where?' hissed Ibiya.

'Keep looking.' They stood waiting like two statues and watched. 'Slowly raise your throwing stick... now!' The shout startled the bird and caused it to fly above the tops of the grass. It kept itself low even in flight and did not emerge far. Ibiya launched the smooth, curved stick hard and fast. The force made him stagger forward and totter, but he fixed his eyes on the throwing stick as it whistled swiftly toward the creature. But the bird didn't stay long in the clear air. It dropped back under cover before the stick could strike. Ibiya shook his head.

'That was unfortunate,' said Dudimose, patting his son's shoulder. 'Quail. They're notoriously difficult. They keep themselves well hidden. Never mind. We'll keep trying.'

Ibiya stalked off to retrieve his weapon. He called back.

'They're also being clever. Using things they know have significance to you: undermining your snake charm; blood in the Nile to remind you of...,' he tactfully moved on, 'and now overwhelming you with sacred frogs that you can't touch. They knew you wouldn't kill a single one, which would make the whole idea ten times more effective.'

Dudimose yelled after him. 'I disagree.' Ibiya stopped and looked back over his shoulder, perplexed. 'You saw total control. I see weakness. To begin an attack and then stop just because your target *asks* you to... there's no strength of will in that! No power. Even the river turned back to water in just one week! My slaves are back to work producing bricks and I've instructed them to replace the lost quota too.' His tone was scornful.

'And Moses *warned* me first; both times. If I chose to demonstrate my power, it would be a sustained pressure. It would not relent until it found the breaking point of...'

'...the Israelite slaves, for example?'

'Exactly! They are lazy, and a drain on our economy. They must be constantly reminded who is in control; who owns them. I assert my power over them daily...'

'I know, Dad. That's what...'

'...and I do not relent, because that would be the worst kind of weakness.' Dudimose paused for effect before his final flourish. 'I do not recognise their god and I told them that. They claimed to show me "that I may know" what he is like. And I know now. Oh, I know.' He chuckled. 'They've shown me exactly what their god is like – weak, Ibiya. He is weak!'

Ibiya turned away. He stooped down to collect his throwing stick, disappearing from view within the tall grasses. Dudimose seethed at the lack of respect his son was showing.

'I have decided not to let them go, Ibiya.'

Ibiya retorted, 'You made a deal, Father. They have kept their side. You owe it...'

'I am not bound by such promises! I am Pharaoh.'

'Model of justice and truth?' Ibiya challenged.

'Free to choose what I will and will not do. Free to change my mind.' He paused. 'And on that subject, I'm removing you from the building project.'

'What? Dad, you can't!'

'I gave you your chance. You did not submit your work to me.'

'The blood... the frogs...!'

'Work continues, Ibiya. I can't have my entire civilisation grind to a halt because of a little inconvenience like that. Sometimes, son, you can be as lazy as those slaves.' Ibiya was speechless. Did his father mean that? 'I have instructed my architect to begin work with my plans. *My* temple will be constructed. You will now oversee the farming community on my behalf.' Ibiya did not argue. He scowled at Dudimose before hanging his head and stalking away, shoving aside the grass with angry blows of his stick. Dudimose called after him, 'Israel will see who has *real* power.'

That night, the king of Egypt should have slept soundly. Work on his temple was underway. The river ran clear, the frogs had died out and at his instruction they had been heaped up downwind and far away from the palace. The streets were clean, his bed was gloriously vacant again, and he had made his decision. The slaves would stay. He had not finished with them yet. He would not let them go, just because Moses had asked him to. He would not be as weak as they were. He was

Pharaoh. Strong. Powerful. In control. But he was sleeping fitfully. Dudimose turned this way and that. His eyelids fluttered. He muttered and moaned. Writhed. Sweated. Shuddered.

In his dream, Moses was charging toward him, wielding his staff like a spear. Dudimose was on his knees, quivering. And he felt so small. Moses seemed to tower above him like a giant. His tunic glowed brilliant white and his eyes burned with intensity. His mouth did not move, but Dudimose could hear his voice. It surrounded him; deep and loud. Echoing. 'Frogs. In your houses. In your bed.' As he watched, aghast, the staff became a row of muddy brown frogs that changed gradually until their skin became moist, shiny green. Each one had enlarged black eyes that bulged out of their heads and tongues that grew longer and longer; extending infinitely, curling around him, sticking to his skin, binding his arms to his sides. More and more followed. Their legs were strong, powerful – propelling them to great heights. He craned his neck to follow their flight over him. As he did so, blood began to ooze from their stretched, shiny skin. It ran down their bodies and dripped from their webbed feet. Dudimose rolled over and writhed on the ground in an attempt to get away, but he could not move. He was stuck. He looked up to see a cobra rising above him; hood open, tongue flickering, ready to strike. Dudimose tried to scream, but his voice did not function. He turned back to see the end of Moses' staff inches from his face. It seemed to suck him towards it. He braced himself against the ground. The cobra lunged at him from behind. Its fangs bared. He tensed, but the stab wound never came. The fangs did not sink in to his flesh. The snake simply slid over his shoulder, its cold skin creepy and cruel. He shuddered. The staff opened wide like a jaw and swallowed it. The frogs followed, twisting and turning, tongues still flicking at him, croaking eerily. Globules of blood leapt up from the ground and also disappeared into the hollow blackness. He felt pulled towards it too. Intrigued by the staff's power, he leaned forward. Moses smashed the staff onto the ground inches from his face, sending violent vibrations across it. Dudimose dived aside. The dust of the ground turned to swarms of gnats and Dudimose found himself surrounded, immersed in a dark, raging cloud. He struggled and spluttered, kicking and flailing and emerged from the incessant buzzing to see bodies strewn everywhere. They were scabby, blistered and tinged with purple. As he swirled around, looking for Moses, he heard a voice. A commanding voice, that seemed to echo through him. He stopped fighting and gave in to its power.

'You *will* know.'

Chapter 15:

Three

Dusk was falling. Moses stood outside the palace gates. Through the gathering darkness he could see Pharaoh standing on his podium, surveying his territory. The sight made Moses' blood boil. His anger was still fresh. The minimum of provocation brought it to the surface again and here, looking at the man who had so callously reneged on his deal, the feelings were powerful. How could he so calmly promise something he did not intend to deliver, just to get what he wanted? He was a cold-hearted man and Moses wished with all his might that he had the power in himself to bring those frogs back. If they came back to life in their half-rotten, foul-smelling, skin-degrading state to haunt Dudimose, that would be even better. He hated the devious, arrogant dictator. Moses had just had to face the elders of Israel and break the news that they would still not be leaving. It had been excruciatingly painful. He'd dashed their hopes. Moses had felt bad. He'd looked bad. Why had God chosen him for this task? Why not someone that Dudimose would respect? Someone he'd respond to? Moses knew he only brought out the worst. Pharaoh hated him. He was glad that God had not told him to face the King of Egypt again today.

Moses kicked the ground. The dust hung in the air around him. He didn't care. He couldn't take any more of this anyway. He turned away from the sight of Pharaoh strutting and started to walk. He knew where he had to go next but he hoped he could perhaps walk off some of his frustration first. He turned a corner, hoping to lose sight of the palace, but it wasn't that easy. Everything here was designed to draw attention to the palace. Every gap between buildings framed it perfectly, drawing attention to its imposing beauty. He kept catching glimpses of it from the corner of his eye. Moses turned again, directly away from the palace so he couldn't possibly see it. He was greeted instead by a statue of Dudimose that looked down on him from ten times his own height. It seemed to mock him. He looked up and turned up his nose. In disgust, he spat on its feet. An unpleasant smell wafted past. He sniffed but it was gone. Moving his eyes away from the statue, he looked at his feet. He'd felt insignificant enough already and this just confirmed his pathetic status. He walked round the giant and carried on, determined to shrug off his foul mood. Pacing the streets, he passed monuments, statues, temples and altars. Dudimose's cartouche greeted him at every turn. The carved oval with the unique hieroglyphic signature kept cropping up to taunt him. Several times, he noticed the strange smell. It came in waves, sometimes distinct and sometimes hardly there. Everywhere he went he was reminded of the power Pharaoh held here. His buildings proclaimed it and his monuments affirmed it. There was proof in the engraved records – lists of victories. He was stupid to think he could fight it. As he walked, the faint smell grew gradually stronger. The further he walked from the palace, the stronger the stench became. He held his breath, his face tightly screwed up in disgust, to avoid inhaling any more than necessary. All thoughts about Pharaoh were now put aside. *What was this smell? Where was it coming from?* His body was now acting instinctively. When he did breathe, his stomach lurched involuntarily and he retched. It was a violent reaction. Moses walked faster. His eyes had started watering. He was heading straight towards Goshen to find Aaron. He had to escape this horror. He turned the next corner, unable to see much through the gathering mass of liquid in his eyes, and stopped dead. He quickly backed away. He'd found the source of the smell. Suddenly it all made sense. Moses was staring at an anarchic pyramid of frogs – unceremoniously dumped; unlike any other pyramid here, its base was not square, it rose unevenly at much too steep an angle and it had been thrown together hastily. The heap was enormous. Frogs had been piled high – legs sprawled, tongues hanging, flesh open, pink and raw. Moses was reviled. He turned and ran. The stench was following him. He couldn't seem to lose it now. His knees ached. He was too old for running like this. He puffed and winced as his feet pounded against the hard ground, jarring his body. As he reached the Goshen border and saw Aaron, he finally slowed. He stooped over, hands on knees, panting for breath. He reflected that he would not wish that experience on anyone and reluctantly admitted to himself that that sentiment even included Dudimose. Even he did not deserve that. He stood up and looked at Aaron who held one hand over his mouth and nose. The smell was still powerful here. *Was it drifting this way on the breeze?* He stood still and inhaled again. It was! Pharaoh had planned the location of his dumping ground, precisely to have this effect. He'd wanted the Israelites to suffer this. The slaves had to walk past that every day to get to work, and endure it when they finally arrived home. And it was as far from the palace as possible. Moses was sickened. Pharaoh was truly vile.

Wordlessly, Aaron nodded to Moses. It was time. Moses sighed. He realised that God perhaps knew him better than he knew himself. Today more than ever, it would be a really bad idea for him to go into the court to face Pharaoh. He was too emotional, too involved. And God had not sent him there. He had given Moses the next step of the plan though – always just the next step. Moses knew he would have done things very differently. This seemed too lenient by far for someone who'd just broken such an important promise. Moses knew God *could* free the entire Israelite population in one go if he chose to. He didn't understand why God *didn't* just do that. Why was he doing things the hard way; deferring to Pharaoh, giving him a chance when it was obvious he'd never agree? Moses sighed again. He was really struggling with his feelings. It felt right that there would be action. He was delighted that Pharaoh would not receive any warning this time. After all, he didn't deserve one. In his heart of hearts Moses knew this was all designed as a demonstration of God's character – 'so you will know'. He knew that God had given *him* a second chance when he'd moaned about not wanting this job. But the human part of him still longed for all this to be punishment – payback for Pharaoh's treatment of Israel – and in his mind no punishment could be severe enough. Someone like that should not receive the same second chance as someone like himself. It wasn't fair!

Aaron touched Moses gently on the shoulder, reminding him it was time. Swallowing his pride, Moses gave Aaron his instructions. Aaron lifted the staff high and thrust it down, plunging it powerfully into the ground. A large cloud of dust rose up around it – thick, gritty, choking dust. Moses coughed, spluttered and wiped his eyes with the back of his hand. Aaron stepped back, away from the staff and the dust now swirling round it. It circled and spiralled up, like a localised sandstorm, growing bigger and thicker all the time. They watched. They could hardly see the staff through the swirling cloud. Particles of dust began to cling together, forming tiny, distinct black dots that danced around one another. There were hundreds of them. Dancing, darting and diving together. They formed a thin veil, blurring the view and causing Moses to blink rapidly. His eyes crossed from trying to focus on them. He swiped his hand through the air in front of his face. In the split second he had a clear view, he saw more and more dust rising from the ground, like mist from the Nile. A low hum started ringing in Moses' ears and as a swarm circled round his head, it became a definite buzz. More and more black bodies twisted and turned in the air. The buzzing grew louder. Moses swiped his hand again and made a grab at the teeming air. He slowly opened his fist. Several tiny black specks lay on his skin. He brought his hand close to his face to inspect them. They had legs like thin strands of hair and transparent wings. He brushed them away. He was beginning to itch.

He walked. The swarms had been attracted to a herd of cattle standing in a nearby field. The gnats were clearly irritating them and they were behaving oddly.

They swished their tails and sent ripples through their skin in an attempt to dislodge the pests before they could gnaw into their thick hide. Moses felt sorry for them. They were making an eerie, low, drawn-out moan. He heard it from where he was. It sounded like they were in pain. The sound unsettled him. He moved cautiously closer. One cow was swinging its head back and forth strangely and another kicked out its leg aggressively. It struck a sleeping calf in the head, knocking it down. Its body fell to the ground with a thud. Its rhythmic breathing stopped abruptly. Its tail stopped flicking and hung limply. Blood oozed from a gash in its head. The blow had taken its young life.

Moses and Aaron continued struggling through the chaotic air towards the palace. Pharaoh had stepped down from his podium into the courtyard. Six servants wafting palm-like fronds surrounded him. But they could not keep the gnats away. His sorcerers were there too, arguing with Pharaoh.

'There's nothing about this written on any papyrus. I couldn't find a single record.'

'Then conjure these creatures yourself!' He was exasperated.

'We have tried, Pharaoh.'

'But already you have stopped?'

'We have tried everything, Pharaoh. I am sorry. I don't know what else…'

'I *need* you to produce gnats. You are employed to do magic at my command. If they can do this, so can you. You are the best sorcerers that Egypt – the *great* civilisation - has to offer.'

'Pharaoh, this is not magic.'

Pharaoh spoke in a low, threatening voice 'What do you mean?' The oldest of his sorcerers stepped forward to defend his young apprentice.

'He is right, Pharaoh. We have nothing that can replicate this. It is definitely not magic as we know it.'

'Then what is behind this?'

The elderly magician spoke in a low whisper, as if afraid to speak it aloud. 'It is the finger of God.'

Pharaoh let out an agonised howl and turned on his heel. He stormed up his steps, leaving his fan-bearers scrabbling to keep up.

Moses turned away, leading Aaron with him. Nothing they could say to Pharaoh could give the message so well. This was the finger of God.

Chapter 16:

Khaldun

A large, elaborately designed, imposing house stood facing the bank of the river Nile. It belonged to the nicest part of the city. The view encompassed the river with the glory of the ships sailing along it and the beauty of the light playing on the water in all its phases throughout each day. The house had its own garden space and more than enough room inside for its occupants. Khaldun's father was a scribe. He was well respected in the community and his position meant many privileges for the family. Still, Khaldun would have gladly given up the fancy adult meals and all the space and toys in return for someone his own age to talk to. He was an only child and there were not many other children living on his street. Most of his day was spent doing lessons and practising the sports that his father believed were so beneficial for him. There was one possession he owned as a result of his father's generous income that he would never give up: his African wildcat.

Khaldun had been allowed to keep the pet because it helped to control rats and other pests that hung around his father's personal grain store. Once, she had killed a poisonous cobra that had found its way into the house, securing her a place in the family for ever. She'd approached it slowly until she was close enough. Then she'd pounced. She'd been rewarded with her own necklace, engraved with hieroglyphics that gave her the name Woserit, which meant mighty woman. And she'd been promised a proper mummification too. Khaldun thought that was much too grandiose and only ever called her Miw-Sher, or kitten, which he much preferred. She jumped onto his lap now as he sat on the front step, wondering what to do with himself. Khaldun stroked the sandy-brown fur on her back as she sat on his lap. He loved the poise with which she usually carried herself, but today her ears were back and her tail shook rapidly. She whined at him. He stopped stroking to check her face. She'd had several red blotches around her eyes, nose and ears this week. They had nasty red bites in the middle. Khaldun knew it was those horrible gnats. The surface of the Nile had been covered in vast clouds of them and they were biting everything in sight. The whole family had been itching like mad. At least they'd been able to stay predominantly indoors, in the cool, but Miw-Sher was still too wild to be contained. She'd gone out as usual by the river and been bitten to pieces. Thankfully, the swarm of biters had moved further down-river now, but Miw-Sher's blotches were only getting worse. He was sure they'd actually got bigger and several of them were now broken and oozing. He held her face gently in his hands to get a closer look. Miw-Sher arched her back and leapt down from his knee. Khaldun was taken aback. She didn't usually behave like that. The bites and sores must be making her irritable. He followed her, looking in each room until he found her on a cushion where she'd curled up. He stroked the back of her head reassuringly. Large clumps of yellow-grey hair came away in his hand and left her sore skin exposed. Eugh! Khaldun wrinkled up his nose in disgust. Despite that, his eyes oozed concern. Was she having some kind of reaction to the gnats?

'What's wrong, Miw-Sher? What is it?' he whispered as he tried to get a closer look. She exhaled with a snort. Her ears and nose looked oddly knobbly. Something was really not right. Her paws were inflamed too, and looked sore. Khaldun gently lifted one foreleg. Miw-Sher had had enough. She finally lashed out. She swiped at his face with her claws, leaving bright red streaks down his left cheek and fled the house.

'Ouch!' he cried. 'Miw-Sher! What was that for? Where have you gone?' Khaldun clutched his cheek. Miw-Sher had never struck out at him before. It just wasn't in her nature. They were the best friends in the world. Khaldun's cheek stung. He felt it burning beneath the palm of his hand as he put gentle pressure on it. 'Miw-Sher!' he called. He felt betrayed. She'd hurt his pride. Khaldun was now more worried about his cat than ever. The feeling was tinged with a sudden wave of sad, empty loneliness. *What if she didn't come back? What would happen to her? And what would he do without her?* Khaldun felt like he'd just lost his only friend.

Part three

Your People.
My People.

Chapter 17:

Father and son

We're trudging to the Nile in silence. Dad's in a bad mood. He's been constantly grumpy since his magicians admitted defeat. He's used to being the most powerful man in Egypt. And Egypt is the most advanced civilisation anywhere. But now that's all being threatened. He's losing his identity to two old men with wooden sticks. And he doesn't like it at all.

I look up. The sky is brilliant blue. The sun is rising above the water. The light makes the ripples glisten and twinkle. But it doesn't help. I don't want to be here. My training has lost its edge now because Dad's so miserable and solemn. He's not involving me. Not explaining anything. He's just instructing me like he would issue orders to a servant. It's like I imagine it would feel to have to do chores. The plans for the temple I drew over and over again, until they were finally good enough for him, have been thrown away without a second thought – and they were so exciting. My temple would have been truly amazing. I shake my head. I still get angry thinking about it. If Dad doesn't want my input, why are we playing this silly training game? Why can't I just enjoy life like I used to? I could be playing senet, or riding one of my donkeys. I have to meet with the farmers instead now. I don't want to. There's nothing I can do to really make a difference to them. They already know what they're doing far better than I do. What do I know about crops and cattle? Dad will just stop me anyway, if I do try to change something. It's pointless. I drag my feet in the dust. All I can think about now is the long day ahead of me. And the rest of the week. I sigh. My mood is beginning to mirror his.

'Dad,' I say, nudging him. He looks up a little blankly, as if I've just disturbed a daydream. He's still sulking. 'Dad!' I say again, tilting my head towards the river. He doesn't even glance in that direction. I nudge him again. 'Dad, look!' He finally looks and sees who I want him to see. He leans in close and grasps my elbow.

'Ibiya,' he whispers. 'I don't need to hear this today. You go on. I'll wait for you in my court.'

It takes a moment for me to realise what he is saying. 'No!' I hiss. I clutch his arm to stop him turning back. 'You're supposed to be teaching me... I can't do this. What would I say?' I'm thinking fast. I need a tactic. Which one would he use? Play on his insecurity. 'Dad, you'll make yourself look weak. You have to...'

Dad turns towards me and holds my face in his hands. He is looking straight into my eyes. I feel like he can read my thoughts. I can feel my cheeks blushing because he's caught me trying to manipulate him. He waits until I'm concentrating and when he speaks his voice is low and quiet. Nobody else can hear it. 'I thought you knew how to handle Moses.'

'Dad, I... no, I don't.'

'Really? Because...'

'I really don't. I need you to stay. Please.' I know I'm begging. I hate being so pathetic but I don't know what else to do.

'Then of course, son, I will stay.' He smiles and my panic eases. My shoulders relax a little. I feel relieved. The thought of facing Moses alone had sent me into a total panic. Dad moves his hands onto my shoulders. 'But, Ibiya,' I look up again. 'I don't want to hear any more from you about what I should have done differently.' I squirm a little. I wish he'd let me go. 'No more muttering. No more questions. No more theories.' He is waiting. I nod. 'I am handling this.'

'Yes.' He releases me and turns to face Moses. I feel much smaller now.

I keep a few steps behind as we approach Moses. I don't want to look at my father. He's just scolded me as if I were a child. It annoys me. I'm supposed to be his heir – in training for his role – and today I'm not even allowed an opinion. I walk, squinting as the glare of sunlight from the surface of the Nile hits my face. I could have put an end to all this nonsense! I stop mid stride, feeling as though I've just been stabbed. Dad just offered me the chance to negotiate with Moses and I turned it down. I'm so stupid! Why didn't I accept the chance? I watch my father walking off ahead of me. Why did he even offer it? He gave up his control and risked me doing things my own way. Why? I glare at his back, horrified. He knew I'd turn it down, didn't he? He saw me as a coward. He'd been so certain I'd act that way, he'd relied on it to make his point. I'm furious! I kick up the dust in my frustration. I storm to catch up. I'm going to tell him exactly how… But we're getting dangerously close to the Nile – and to Moses. Reluctantly, I put on my public face and draw myself up tall. I know when to hold it in well enough by now, but my anger burns inside and I feel a total fraud.

Moses gives a funny little bow. It's as if he's not sure whether he should keep up the pretence of respect or not. I scowl. Any other day, I'd probably find it funny, but I'm in too bad a mood. My father must be finding it insulting too. This, after all, is the man who recently unleashed an army of gnats – without a single word of warning. I get the impression that Moses is feeling uncomfortable. It occurs to me that it must have taken a lot of courage for him to come here to face Dad again today. The sort of courage I wish I possessed. And he's persistent. I'm looking at him, and though he is old and unsure of himself, I feel an unexpected wave of respect.

Immediately, I force myself to look away. I'm feeling guilty. Dad has only just reprimanded me for having too many of my own thoughts. I'm supposed to be on his side. It's the last place I feel like being, but 'Control begins with self-control,' he's always told me 'and self-control begins with your mind.' So I try. Pharaoh good, Moses bad, I remind myself. I repeat it in my head. We are waiting for someone to start the exchange, holding out in yet another battle of wills; my mind drifts. What would I have done if I'd taken that opportunity? Am I on his side? I admit I haven't exactly been supportive. I suppose I never realised that my dad, King of Egypt, needed anyone's support. Or wanted it. He'd always been so strong and sure of himself. I look at him now and realise, for the first time in my life, that he's just an older version of me. I swallow hard. One day, I'll be in his position, making tough decisions every day – and I know without question that I won't have all the answers. Why do I expect him to? It makes me feel a little sorry for him. I force my facial muscles back into place. I can't afford to betray what I'm thinking. I can't even imagine Dad's reaction if he knew his own son felt sorry for him. Anyway, I'm still too angry with him to let myself have too much sympathy. He's just played me like a game of senet. Oh, why can't I be playing senet now, instead of standing here? Still, this couldn't be easy for him either.

'Thus says the Lord, "Let my people go, that they may serve me. For if you do not let my people go, behold, I will send swarms of insects on you and on your servants and on your people and into your houses; and the houses of the Egyptians will be full of swarms of insects, and also the ground on which they dwell."' He takes a deep breath. '"But on that day I will set apart the land of Goshen, where my people are living, so that no swarms of insects will be there, in order that you may know that I, the Lord, am in the midst of the land. I will put a division between my people and your people. Tomorrow this sign will occur."'

Take your people, I want to scream! That'd get back at Dad. He wouldn't get his silly temple built and he'd see I'm not the coward he thinks I am. But I don't speak because I've been warned, and I'm too afraid of actually upsetting my father. Perhaps I am a coward. No, he's already having a difficult time, I remind myself. And I'm on his side – being supportive. He doesn't say anything either. Moses leaves. What does my father plan to do? Does he have a strategy now? Does he want my help? I bite my tongue. I concentrate hard on not letting any words tumble out of my mouth but my eyes give me away. They are searching Dad's face for clues. His expression is blank, as ever, and tells me nothing. Eventually, he takes pity. He rolls his eyes at me.

'I don't plan to give in, Ibiya.'

'Why, Dad?' I try hard to make it sound like an enquiry and not a challenge.

'Because, Ibiya.'

Because? That's not an answer! I wait. I bite my lip to force myself not to ask. I tap my thumbs impatiently together.

'Because, I don't want to.'

'You don't want to!' That slipped out before I could stop it. My anger is still hot.

He lowers his voice to a whisper. 'I have realised, and will admit to you – only to you and this is not for repeating – that this god apparently has more power than I do. My magicians simply were not able to reproduce the gnat trick. The competition is over. They won. But... the key thing, Ibiya, is that they are still only asking. And, as it is a request, it is quite acceptable for me to decline.'

'Yes, except...'

'We have survived everything else. We will survive a few more insects!' His patience is wearing out.

I am stumped. I start walking towards the Nile. My father matches my pace.

'Do you know what makes me really cross, Ibiya?' I think. Not for too long, because he's going to tell me anyway, but I try to give the impression that I'm considering the question.

'No, I...'

'That he comes into my territory and dares to call my slaves his people. They are mine!'

'Yes. You need them for your building projects.' I roll my eyes.

'That's correct.' He pauses, and then adds, 'Ibiya, what have you done to familiarise yourself with the methods employed in our farming community?'

I hesitate. The truth is I haven't done anything. I've been putting it off. Farming doesn't interest me and I'm still sore about not being allowed to pursue the project I was really enjoying.

'Ibiya?'

'I... I have... I intend to meet with the workers this afternoon. I'll get a general overview and then... I'll be able to allocate time to each of the important areas and...'

'You've wasted your time so far?' I hang my head. I'm ashamed, but also still angry more than anything else. 'I know that you are cross with me.' I look up. 'You think I should have built my temple according to your plans.' I nod tentatively. 'Perhaps I should have. But the thing is, Ibiya, I was not expecting so much from you. You have to remember that my priority is to train you. I thought, wrongly, that the field of architecture would provide you a significant challenge. It took me years to understand many of the intricacies of good planning. Your initial attempt shows a real flair.' I'm confused. He seems to be complimenting me. If my plans were that good, why didn't he use them? 'You surprised me. I think you have a natural talent which means that when your turn comes, though there will still be a lot for you to learn along the way, you will pick it up with relative ease. That's why I have chosen instead to develop your skills in an alternative area.'

'So my reward for success is to be worked harder?'

'Be careful. Your attitude is very negative.'

'I have no interest in farming.'

'I have no natural interest in many things, Ibiya, but I have developed them. A Pharaoh has to be able to make judgements in all aspects of Egyptian life. To do that he must know everything there is to know about each of them. You can either be miserable about it, or try to enjoy the experience. Like it or not, this is your future role. And my job is to prepare you for it.'

Chapter 18:

Four

I'm barely awake. I'm much more aware than I want to be though. Something is droning in my ears. I try to shut it out. It's early. My eyes are still firmly closed and I'm still half-immersed in a dream, but my head flicks from one side of my body to the other, jolting me. I try to keep it still so that I can get comfortable and doze off but it's not working. The noise won't leave me alone. My neck twitches again. As I slowly, reluctantly, become more aware of myself, I notice an itchy patch on my cheek. I rub it with the back of my hand and try to sleep again. I wriggle until I'm comfortable and relaxed. As I begin to settle, something on my forehead tickles. It really annoys me. I sleepily scratch the spot and roll over. What is that humming? It's constant! Ignore it, Ibiya. I concentrate on my breathing and try to remember my dream. I really don't want to begin my day yet. It's much too early for that and I have lost sleep to catch up on. I lie for a while, gradually beginning to feel heavy again. My thoughts are slipping away. I don't know whether I'm asleep or awake. Without realising what I'm doing, my arm brushes the top of my head. I drag it across my scalp to relieve another itch. Then my sluggish brain begins to creep into action. What's going on? My sheet has slid off my shoulder and now that feels itchy too. It tickles, as if a feather had brushed it. My skin crawls. I yawn and open my eyes a fraction. I turn to pull the sheet back and look at my bare shoulder. I stare, still in that awkward position, not moving. My eyes are bleary. I blink. It's not yet dawn and the room is dim. As my eyes adjust, the shadowy blur on my shoulder comes into focus. Eugh! My heart leaps into my throat. A large, black, scary-looking fly is standing on my bare skin! Six spindly, black legs splay out from its dark, hairy body. The tiny claws pinch my skin. Its eyes are large and red on the sides of its head and seem to look round me. Jagged bluish wings protrude at odd angles from its back. It is ugly. I gasp, cough and feel something gunky come up into the back of my throat. I cough again to clear my throat but I can't dislodge the lump. I swallow it back down. I feel it travelling slowly inside me. I cough again, harder this time and the foul, bitter tasting lump propels itself up onto my tongue. I push it to the front of my mouth and onto my lips. I wipe with a finger and cringe at the mess of black gunk I see. Congealed fly. I'm beginning to understand that hum now. As I stare, the fly on my shoulder lowers its head to probe my skin. No you don't. I flick it hard and watch it spiral through the air and fly away.

A scream erupts from me before I can stop it. I cower under my sheet, shaking a little from the shock. I've just jumped out of my skin. My eyes scan the room, taking in the horrific sight. Every surface in the room is crawling with hairy, black flies. The walls are thick with them. There are so many that they're crawling over each other and I can't see the white plaster surface of the wall, only a shifting black mass of insects. The volume of their buzzing seems magnified now that I've seen how many there are. It's relentless and infuriating. The ceiling is the same. I'm craning my neck to look, though I really don't want to. Several flies break off from the horde and dart around in the air above me. They dodge and weave erratically to avoid one another in the confined space. I wrinkle up my nose. This is disgusting. I'm coughing again, more violently this time, clearing another bitter lump from my lungs. There's still more in my throat. I can feel them lurking there. How many of these creatures are in there? Did I swallow them in my sleep or did they just crawl in? I shudder. I sit up – slowly – and look down. The floor is crawling. I'm stranded on my low bed. The thought of lowering my bare foot into that... sinister black sea... to be bitten to pieces sends shivers through me. It's too horrible for words. What am I going to do? I have an urge to protect myself from this blight. I grab the edge of my sheet to cover myself again. I pull it to my chin. A louder hum rings in my ears as a thick cloud of flies rises from it into the air. They've been sharing my bed. I scream again, louder than before, and inhale a mouthful from the swarm I've just disturbed. The insides of my cheeks are crawling, itching – my mouth is full. I can't breathe in or I'll swallow them, I can't shut my mouth or they'll be trapped. I claw them out, trying not to breathe. I scrape them from my tongue with my fingernails. Pain shoots through one side of my face. They're biting. I gasp in pain, gag on my mouthful and end up with flies in the top of my nose. I snort, desperate to breathe again. I feel invaded, choked and sore. I hold one nostril, expelling air from the other, trying to clear it. It's not working. I have to get out of here. I need to get away. Tears trickle down my cheeks. I quickly wipe them away. Don't be so pathetic, Ibiya. But I feel pathetic. I still can't breathe properly. I'm swallowing more by the minute. I'm in a nightmare. Awake, alert and very scared. I want to get up, but I find myself paralysed; not knowing what to do next, unable to move.

Think, Ibiya. Where are your sandals? You can do this. They're only flies. I scan the room, unable to see anything but the shifting mass of black. Dad, I blame you for this. I close my eyes and think back, trying to remember – under the bed. They're under the bed. I look down and cringe. Why did you do this to me, Dad? I prepare myself, hold my breath and plunge my hand down. My fingers touch the flies. My hand sinks in. The sea of insects feels cold, rough and alive. Several break off from the mass, dart off into the air and circle my face. I shake my head to keep them away. One plunges into my right eye. I blink furiously. I can't see. Everything is a blur. My other hand is still immersed in flies. They're crawling over me, climbing up my arm, pinching, biting. I'm fumbling around for my sandals, wiping my eye with the back of my other hand. I sneeze. I can feel my anger rising. Why is this happening? I know the answer. I know who is to blame. Great Pharaoh. Powerful Pharaoh. Model of justice and truth. Protector of Egypt. My fingers clutch the leather of one sandal and I yank it up. Flies disperse in a droning haze. I slap at my arm to stop the biting. Squashed black blobs speckle my hand. There's nowhere to wipe them so I shake it rapidly in mid air. *You're not protecting us from this, are you?* I'm so cross. Anger is taking over from the shock. My skin is burning. I look down at my arm, which is red and blotchy from the bites. I rub it to try to soothe the burning. Where are all the frogs when you need them? As if I don't know. My eye is still streaming. I wipe the tears away with the back of my hand and use my middle finger to drag the sleep-coated mess from the inside corner. *All you had to say was, 'Yes, Moses. You can go.' How hard could it be to make sure they came back? You have an army, don't you? A great and powerful army. Why are we going through all this…?* I puff and plunge my hand down a second time, much more swiftly than before. I don't waste any time. I grab, pull and shake the other sandal. I do not want to give those flies time to latch on to me again.

I'm finally dressed and out of that dreaded room but I haven't found relief anywhere. The flies are literally everywhere. I can't see far ahead because the air is black and every surface in Egypt is crawling with them. Walls, buildings, even statues have taken on a sinister appearance today. My feet are crunching with every step. I haven't seen dad yet. I was told he was in an emergency meeting with his priests. I decided not to join him as I hadn't been formally invited. It's best the way I feel today. I need to calm down first and I'm heading to the one place where that may actually be possible.

At the border of Goshen, I gawp in disbelief. I am standing, still surrounded by flies. They permeate the air around me. They are crawling inside my clothes, on my skin and through my hair. I tear at the skin on my back, writhing and contorting, unable to reach the spot. It's burning. But looking ahead, I can see air as clear as the Nile water – as clear as it used to be anyway, before the blood and the dead fish. If I take one more step, I will be able to see clearly, to breathe freely and to relieve the creeping sensation on my skin. Perhaps even hear myself think again. The division is total. It's awesome. I fully expected to find that Moses had been truthful; that his god could keep the flies out of Goshen. After all, he was able to kill off the frogs exactly when dad asked him to. I just assumed his control over place would be as accurate as his control over time. Even so, standing on the border takes my breath away. I close my mouth and slowly stretch out one leg. I'm hesitant; a little unsure of what will happen to me if I cross the line. Perhaps the flies will stay with me. I belong in Egypt after all. Would I then be responsible for polluting this haven? I look back. People in the streets of Egypt are hunched over, scuttling around. Their faces are anguished. Their hands flap and their arms flail, trying to clear their faces. I have a choice. If that's the alternative, then I'm going to risk it. Perhaps it is selfish, but I'm angry with Dad. I don't feel like staying to support him through this. He's done this to those people; people who look to him for everything. And he's done this to me – his firstborn son.

I take one step. One little step and it's like being in a totally new world. Flies that clung to me simply hang in the air where I was standing. They join the swarms. The incessant tickling motion over my body stops instantly. I can see clearly. There is an invisible wall marking the beginning of Pharaoh's territory and the end of the Israelite's land. It's as if a physical barrier is keeping them out. I'm on the right side of it and it feels so good. I breathe deeply. I can do that now without risking

inhaling lungfuls of tiny pests. It's refreshing. I take
several lungfuls and erupt in another bout of coughing.
I spit out another few mouthfuls of insects. My throat is
beginning to feel clear again. I feel alive instead of
stifled. I stand still, just enjoying the clear air and the
lack of small, irritating creatures on and around me,
buzzing in the inside of my ears. Then I examine my skin
for more blotches. It's red and horrible. When I look up
again, I notice the stream of Israelite slaves making the
transition in the opposite direction. They've seen me too
and they're not happy about it. Several men are huddled
together, muttering and pointing at me. Before I know
it, a row of large Israelite men walk straight at me. I look
for an escape route. I don't want to go back. I see the
disgust on their faces as they approach the wall. I brace
myself. They're getting close. I duck and attempt to dive
under their linked arms but they close the gap. I'm
swept back across the border with them. There's horror
on their faces as they enter the teeming air. I'm
deposited back where I belong – in Egypt. I pull myself
up tall, determined not to let them see how angry I feel,
and watch a dramatic change overcome their bodies as
they stoop and cower to adapt to the onslaught. They
have no choice but to be here. They have work to do.
They're not giving me one either. I can't blame them.
They see me and think of my father. He's forging ahead
with his temple project in spite of everything and he

certainly hasn't lightened the load of his slaves. As far as they're concerned, that's where I stand too. Do I? Is this what I'd do in his place? I don't think so, but I'm beginning to doubt myself. Am I really any better or will I turn out just like him? Hard and uncaring. If only I could be stronger. I sigh. The Israelites have the hope of escape at the end of the day. Tonight, they'll return to this haven. If only I didn't look so Egyptian – so much like my dad. I stand, surrounded again by buzzing beasts, crawling over my scalp, creeping down my back, and gaze longingly into Goshen. Something catches my attention in the distance. I watch closely until I'm certain, straining to see through the movement. Among the hordes of Israelites are two faces I recognise. Moses. Aaron. They're coming into Egypt too, and I think I know where they're going. Has Dad realised his mistake? Is he ready to end this? They're going to the palace. They've been summoned. My frown fades. I join the crowd, keeping a little way behind Moses and Aaron so that they will not see me. If they are going to the palace, this may end soon. There is hope for me too!

I've lost them. The combination of the thick air and the hordes of slaves has stopped me from keeping up. It doesn't really matter. I know where they're heading. Where else? I dodge out from behind a group of slaves, complaining bitterly about the conditions, and skirt around the edge of the procession. I storm ahead swiping flies from my vision this way and that with swift movements of my arms. I pass the statue of my father – his previous masterpiece – which now, rather than grand and inspiring, is black and creepy. It makes him appear quite menacing. I can't look at it. I approach the palace courtyard from a side entrance and see that the meeting has already begun.

'It is not right to do so.' It's Moses and his voice is stronger and firmer than I'd expect. 'The sacrifices we make would be an abomination to the Egyptians.' My father does not respond. Apparently that does not concern him even slightly. What's going on? What has he said? 'If we make sacrifices to the Lord our God where the Egyptians can see us, will they not then stone us?' Again there's no immediate answer. *If we sacrifice...* *Dad's allowing that then – wow! But...* 'where they can see us... stone us.' As I stand hidden in the shadow of a column, swatting flies with my hand and repeating the words over to myself it dawns on me – he's still not letting them go! I'm outraged. All this and he's still not granting their request. He wants them to sacrifice here, in Egypt! Wow! Moses is right. Egyptians would stone him. The Israelites sacrifice cattle; the bull is sacred here. It would be the biggest insult imaginable. Moses continues tentatively. I can see he is trying to judge how far to push my father. 'We must go three days' journey into the wilderness and sacrifice to the Lord our God as he commands us.'

Father rolls his eyes. He sighs loudly. 'I will let you go that you may sacrifice to the Lord your God in the wilderness. Only you shall not go... Very Far Away. Make supplication for me.' His staccato conveys his impatience and emphasises this latest condition to the deal.

He is turning away. His command is intended to conclude the meeting but Moses speaks again. 'Behold, I am going out from you, and I shall make supplication to the Lord that the swarms of insects may depart from Pharaoh, from his servants, and from his people tomorrow.' Dad nods once. Again he tries to turn away. 'Only do not let Pharaoh deal deceitfully again in not letting the people go to sacrifice to the Lord.'

My father's jaw drops. Moses has just openly mocked him. He is at a loss for words.

Chapter 19:

Warning

'Dad, what is it? Your messenger just found me.'

'Where have you been today?'

'I was with the farmer who oversees the region, discussing the crops…'

Dad nods with an approving smile. That's good. I've done something right. 'Sit down, Ibiya. You've had a long day.'

I do. I'm glad of the opportunity to rest. I've been on my feet all day, learning the layout of the crops and meeting all the livestock. The sprint back to the palace used up the last of my energy. I realise how hungry I am. I slump onto the cushion and catch my breath. Dad is watching me. He looks serious. It's evening but he sits upright in a formal chair. He's still in work mode.

'How was your meeting with the priests?' He looks as though he's forgotten it had even happened. Apparently that's not what he summoned me to discuss. He seems to consider his response for a while, stroking his chin.

'I questioned them for several hours. I covered every aspect of their work. They each gave satisfactory answers. I could find no fault. So, I'm puzzled as to what could have upset the gods so much. Why do you think they are allowing all this, Ibiya?'

The question takes me by surprise. I hesitate. I hadn't really thought of it that way. I'd thought it was Dad doing all the allowing. 'You think they are allowing it then?'

'Of course they're allowing it. For whatever reason, they've decided not to protect me from this Israelite onslaught. My job now is to work out how we are failing them.'

'What if you're not failing them?'

'That's preposterous, Ibiya! What a ridiculous thing to say.' His eyes are piercing. 'What reason would they then have to turn against me; against my Egypt?'

'What if they're not able to protect you?'

Dad looks at me oddly, as though he doesn't quite recognise me. His brows are furrowed and his head is tilted to one side. He shakes the thought out of his mind. I yawn. 'I've had another visit from our Israelite friends.' He is matter of fact: hard to read. I look up.

'You didn't send for me.'

'I didn't know where you were. And it transpires that you were busy in any case. You must have a lot on your plate with the farm supervisors, discussing the season. Are you happy with their work?' I'm confused. I stretch out and rip a chunk from a loaf on the table next to me. He sent for me and now seems to want to avoid the topic. I chew on a mouthful. I decide to play it safe and just answer his question.

'With their work: yes. They are tireless. I never realised how much goes into producing food of this quality. However, we do have some serious issues with the barley crop.' He nods for me to continue. 'It went without water for a whole week, which weakened it significantly. The flies then laid their eggs in the soil, which have hatched and the larvae are systematically attacking the stems of the crop.'

Dad nods again. I'm not sure if he was listening or not. I change tack. 'What did they say? Have they changed their demands at all?'

'No son, it was the usual. "Let my people go that they may serve me. If you refuse… blah, blah, blah… the hand of the Lord will come with a very severe pestilence…"'

'They're angry with you then? I thought they would be. You agreed to let them go after the flies were dealt with and…'

'And they did not learn their lesson from the frog scenario!' Suddenly he's come alive. His eyes glisten and his face is animated. His passion is written on his face. It's clear this is what he wanted to get to. He's been bursting to say what's coming next. 'They should use their power to leverage me – force me to give them what they are asking for. They could have refused to stop the flies until I let them go, but...'

I swallow a half-chewed mouthful to interrupt him. 'And would you then let them?'

'Of course not!' He's stunned and looks at me as if that was the most obvious thing in the world.

'So what difference does it make, how they...?'

'If we really must have this battle, I'd prefer a worthy opponent – a bit of a challenge.' He puts on his bored voice. 'They simply ask for freedom and do whatever I ask to get it. It's pathetic. They expect that I will be falling over myself to help them after they've met my demands. But the frogs are gone. And now the flies are gone. What reason do I have to let them go now? I cannot respect pushovers who act like that.'

'No reason!' I'm leaning forward now, waving the chunk of bread about as I express myself. 'Dad, if even a few frogs had been left alive, then the flies would not have thrived. The population would have been kept in check by the frogs. They would not have been able to destroy my barley harvest the way they have. My farmers slaved to recuperate those plants after their drought when the river turned to blood. They have tended and nursed them back to health, only to see them destroyed by millions of horrible crawling maggots. You had the power to prevent that, Dad!'

'Calm down, Ibiya. We still have the flax and the wheat to come. And all the wonderful fruits after that! Barley was a small sacrifice for the greater good.'

I can't believe I'm hearing this. I grit my teeth. First my temple plans and now my crops – nothing I do is valued. I cannot get my father to listen. If I can't, how must his people feel?

He chuckles to himself. I slump back on my cushion. 'I love my power, Ibiya. I say, "No more flies, please." They obey me.' He smiles. 'Life is good.'

I'm trying hard to understand, but he makes it so difficult for me. 'Yes. The flies are gone, but that does not bring back my harvest. The frogs are gone, but we're still dealing with the smell from their rotten bodies. You're not thinking about the chain of effects all of this has for your people. Now they're going to bring pestilence: very severe pestilence on... what exactly? Because you are still refusing to give up three days' worth of labour. Three days!'

'We'd lose seven at the very least – three days there, three back and one for their pathetic ritual. That's an entire week, Ibiya!' He's unbelievable. I slam down the squashed and crumbled bread.

'It's still just a few days in the great scheme...' Dad shakes his head.

'You still think they'd come back, don't you?'

I look at him. 'You still think they wouldn't? They've done everything else you've asked of them.'

He ignores that. 'But you are rightly concerned about the effects.' I nod. 'I am too, Ibiya. I want you to know I am always considering them. That's why I asked you to come this evening. The pestilence they spoke of will be on the livestock in the field. Moses listed a few: horses, camels, donkeys and I think he mentioned the herds and flocks too. He says he's going to bring this tomorrow.'

I'm lost for words.

'And he probably will, because I am not letting them go after all the hours' work they've cost me during this ridiculous drama. I thought you should know so that you can prepare.'

'My livestock! You've given me responsibility for all the farming in Egypt. Crops and animals, and now you've agreed to let them all be...' I'm on my feet. Dad is calm.

'It's very interesting. Moses named the precise date, and he also specifically said that the livestock of Israel will not be affected. I don't see how that's possible because any kind of disease would usually spread. Perhaps this time he's finally promised more than he can deliver. I knew eventually he'd trip himself up. I'm looking forward to it.'

'You had no right to make that decision without me! It was mine to make. I'm now expecting a direct attack on my livestock while you sit in the palace unaffected by it all.'

He flashes me a warning glance. I'm treading close to the line.

'You are wrong, Ibiya. Do not presume to build your statue before you wear your crown. All decisions in Egypt are mine to make. I will not be "unaffected". I expect you to keep me informed of how you are managing the situation. I want regular updates. Now sleep; you have a lot to prepare for before the morning.'

'How can I be expected to maintain the whole system of farming if you refuse to protect it? You are standing back and allowing my work to be attacked!'

'I am protecting the farm land. I'm protecting our assets – slaves – that belong to Egypt. Those assets benefit the whole of Egyptian life. Without them, there'd be no dykes to irrigate your fields. I am also protecting my right to make decisions here without being manipulated and bullied; by them, or by you.'

I'm pacing. I can't stand this. He makes it all sound so good and logical, but it's wrong, so wrong. I just wish I had the words to make him see that. I can't make him understand what his actions are doing outside of this palace. He won't see it. I stomp away. Then I think better of it and decide to say what's on my mind after all. Perhaps my raw frustration will speak to him more than any reasoned argument I could have constructed. I turn back and pace towards him. I stand closer than usual, invading his comfort zone a little. I open my mouth. But I'm too late. He's anticipated my move and blocks it.

'Ibiya. It's really encouraging to see that you're taking your new role so seriously. I commend your speech on behalf of the farming community. I know you cannot really feel it. You said yourself you have no interest in farming.'

I close my mouth; turn on my heel and leave. I feel like banging my head several times against a column, or perhaps his.

Chapter 20:

Five

I'm leaning against a wall; waiting. My legs are stretched out, arms folded comfortably across me, and my chin is resting on my chest; just waiting. Something's going to happen. But what? When? I can only wait. This latest curse is an odd one, in that it seems to be having no immediate effect. Have Moses and his brother got it wrong? Have they forgotten something? Perhaps. But I doubt it. I look relaxed but I'm constantly alert. Aware of everything that's going on around me, ready to spring into action as soon as I'm needed. I tilt my head a little like a dog pricking up its ears. The sheep's bleating has changed. I'm listening carefully now because it's taken on a slightly different tone. There's no sign of any predator but I'm certain they sound distressed. I spring up from my position and break into a run. I hurry, jump over the water channel and almost lose my footing as I land. My hands instinctively fly out as I sprawl forwards. I stumble and land on my knees. The impact jars through my legs. But I haven't got time to think about myself. I pull myself to my feet and brush off the dust. I look up. The sheep are walking over to me. They seem curious about what I'm doing, but otherwise they're behaving normally. Did I imagine their complaints? I'm sure I didn't. I feel like I'm going crazy. I look around.

Most of the cows are now lying down, huddled together. Don't overreact, Ibiya. It's nothing unusual. I stroll casually over, fighting to convince myself I don't need to race again. I'm trying to keep calm. If only my mind would do the same. I wouldn't expect them to sleep at this time of day, and it's the dry season so they can't be anticipating rain either. It's not a dramatic change, but it's definitely something. Their low complaining lament is unsettling me. Should I go for help? I'm not an expert after all.

Before I make my decision, help arrives. Two experienced farm workers have heard the cattle and are sprinting up the hill. I stand like a statue among the sheep. They swerve into the field and begin their professional examination of a large muscular cow. It moans and pulls away as they check its ears, its mouth and its eyes. It takes all their strength to hold it. I can't watch. I turn and crouch on the ground in front of a small, anguished sheep. I look into its eyes. *Are you in pain? What's happening little one?* It bleats at me. I'm bewildered. I don't know where to start.

'Over here!' The farmer arrives and pushes me gently aside. The sheep bleats again. It's call is noticeably weaker this time.

'It's a breathing thing. He's not in pain, just a bit lethargic – under the weather. Like the rest of them.' He

141

tilts his head back towards the cows. 'Same with them. Their breathing's not right.'

'What can we...?' He shakes his head and shrugs.

'Are they eating?'

'Not really.'

'Let's check those horses. I put them in the field beyond the fig this morning.' I trudge behind him in silence, thinking. The expert can't explain their odd behaviour. But I think I can. I look up at the fig tree on top of the hill. It's wide, low branches shelter the dozen or so horses. These are some of Egypt's best. I shake my head. These creatures have been sentenced. I doubt there's anything any of us can do. Halfway there, a donkey passes us. He looks just like one of mine. Perhaps it's a relative. He lets out a loud bray. I wince. It's rasping. It sounds like his airway is blocked. I look to the farmer in concern. He sighs.

'He's old. Whatever this is, he might not...'

'Don't say that! Don't... there must be something...'

'I don't know.'

I pat the donkey between his ears and deliberately avoid looking into his mournful brown eyes. I can't bear it. I stand and watch him as he staggers past. I trudge on. After a few steps, I stop and look back over my shoulder. There's a lump in my throat. This is so unfair. I feel like shouting. What have these creatures done to deserve this?

'Ibiya!'

I run to catch up. Before I even reach the horse, I skid to a halt. My stomach churns. My eyes are wide and disbelieving.

'That's impossible. I've been checking all morning. I was here not very long ago. Everything was fine.' The horse's side has a large open gouge. It is red, sore and weeping. Blood trickles through its hair, matting it together in sticky clumps. I shake my head. I'm fighting a lost cause. I know nothing about treating animals. It wouldn't matter if I did. They've been sentenced... to death. I stare at the horse, once strong, powerful and athletic – arresting in battle – now weak, wobbly and frail. My heart sinks with the realisation that there is nothing I can do to stop this escalating. It's out of my hands. The magicians couldn't produce gnats. Nothing could stop the frogs. What made me think I could prevent this? The flies had been an assault on my senses; irritating, disgusting. This was an attack on my heart. I hadn't been here long, but I'd started to really care for these animals. I knew their habits, their personalities and their strengths. I feel myself choking up. I swallow hard and put a hand on the horse's back. It turns its head and whinnies. It shows me its teeth. I force myself to smile back. Poor creature.

The sheep lay shaking on the ground. Clumps of wool fall away in my hand as I check his breathing. It's shallow and weak. Its eyes are dull and blood is seeping from open sores, similar to the one on the horse. All the creatures have them now. They appeared so suddenly. The loss of blood is making them cold and sapping their energy. Shivering and shaking from the breathing difficulties, they whimper. I feel like we should be doing something; treating the sores, stemming the flow of blood. Keeping the animals warm and fed – something, anything. But I know that it's impossible. There are so many animals developing identical conditions and it's all happening so fast.

I remember my promise to Dad and, with a lump in my throat, I signal for a messenger to go to the palace. 'Please inform the Pharaoh that the animals are dying – all of them. There's nothing we can do.' I close my eyes and wish this situation away. When I finally open them again, the shaking and wheezing has stopped. The sheep is dead. I stand up and walk down the hill. Halfway to the stable compound, I pass a scruffy heap lying across the road; the donkey. I look away, step round the body and break into a run.

The fields are littered with carcasses. That means loss of labour, loss of food and other products, and masses of clearing up to do. Mountains of rotting cow are going to be much less easy to hide than mountains of frogs. I feel so helpless against this Israelite god especially without my dad's help. Hot angry tears run down my cheeks.

Chapter 21:

Six

I'm sitting on the steps with my arms folded across my knees. My head rests on my arms. My whole body feels heavy and tired. A stream of thoughts fills my mind. Images of the week keep coming back to me. The horrible gouges, weeping blood and gunk, and the quivering bodies, shuddering with each shallow breath. I can still hear the low moaning of the cows and the donkey's last rasping breaths. I sigh. It's too much. I can't get rid of the images: eyes shut; eyes open; they're still there. This entire tragedy happened in just a few short days; too fast for me, for anyone, to do anything to stop it. There's been one grotesque development after another. Today was worse – more terrible – than anything else so far. Unpleasant smells and irritating flies are one thing, but when animals are distressed and harmed – and end up dead because of it – that's something else altogether. It's wrong. And Moses stayed to watch it all unfold. That's horrible, morbid. I feel repulsed by that. How could anyone want to watch that kind of suffering? Why? I don't understand. I feel like I should cry about it. Like it would be good for me to relieve the tension, but the tears won't come. I'm too angry, still in shock. I scratch my arm.

Dad arrives on his podium. I don't hear him. I'm just somehow aware that he's there now. I can tell I'm not alone anymore. I don't want him to see me like this. I need him to know how strong I can be. I lift my head. But the effort and the sorrow and the confusion is too much for me. I can't think of anything to say.

'Ibiya.'

I don't move. I can't even begin to open up. I don't want to talk. Instead I scratch the spot on my arm again.

'Ibiya, I'm sorry.'

I choke back a snort of laughter. Of all the things I expected my dad to say at this moment, that wasn't it. I search for an appropriate response. He doesn't move. He stays on his podium. I don't either. I stay on the step, keeping my face turned away. I need that privacy.

'I am sorry, Ibiya. I know you cared. I know you wouldn't have let things happen that way. I know...'

'Why did you?' My voice is too quiet but he heard me speak. He waits. I scratch my arm, clawing absent-mindedly at the stubborn itch. I can't get rid of it. 'Why did you do it that way?' I say again, my voice stronger now.

He breathes deeply. He's thoughtful, taking the question seriously. 'Ibiya, I don't expect you to understand this. You're so young. Everything is still ink on papyrus to you.' He gulps. 'I'm not sure I know anymore why I'm doing what I'm doing. I just know I have to stand up to this. I have to remain strong.'

I shake my head. 'Dad...'

'I know, Ibiya. I know. You're hurting. Today was tough for you. I hate that what I have to do affects you that way. I don't want you...'

'Do you? Do you really? It feels as though you'll say anything to...'

'You're my son! How could you ever think that I...' his voice cracks. Is he acting? Or could he actually mean this? I can't tell anymore. I don't know how my own father really feels about me. My arm still itches. I rub it slowly with my palm. Nothing seems to soothe it.

'Come here, Ibiya. My son.'

I don't move. He can come to me.

'Ibiya... I...' he trails off.

I still don't move. I don't even look round. He waits. I'm holding my ground and this time I don't intend to give in. If he means what he says, he'll come down from his podium – would that even occur to him? Just a few steps – and take me in his arms. Show me he means it.

I hear shuffling footsteps approach.

'Pharaoh.'

'Well?'

'Untouched. Not a scratch on any of them.'

'You checked all the livestock?'

'All of them, Pharaoh. Each animal of every breed. Not one is affected.'

'Thank you. You may go.'

The messenger leaves. Dad sighs.

'Well, Moses was accurate again.' I assume this is directed at me. 'It seems Israel's livestock were exempt. Their god certainly is good to his people.'

'Better than you are to yours.' I retort. 'Did you just say "his" people?'

'My slaves! Their god is good to my slaves.'

I don't hear anything after that. He doesn't speak, doesn't move around. I'm not sure if he's even still there.

As I sit, head still resting wearily on my arms, I hear more people approach. I feel tension in the air. I know it's Moses. Moments pass. Nothing is spoken. As I listen to them leave, wondering what just happened, I lift my head and feel a fine mist fall over me. It's like rain, but dry. Powdery. My skin is coated in a dusty layer. I don't care. I stay where I am. I don't want to see him again today.

I realise I'm scratching my arm again. I'm horrified by what I see when I look down. Where did that come from? I stifle a scream. My heart is suddenly racing. What is it? My lungs are working faster than usual. I can't take my eyes off the blistering, blackened patch of skin on my arm. It's flaky, itchy, and it looks disgusting.

'Dad!' I look round, craning to see if he's still there. What is this thing on my arm? As I scramble to my feet, I notice for the first time that there are several more of them on my legs and my other arm. Small blisters that are black to their core. Immediately I see them, they begin to itch too. And my neck. How many are there? I wonder. How long have they been there? Where did they come from?

'Dad!' I call again, and sprint up the steps, two at a time to the podium. He joins me as if from the shadows and opens his arms to embrace me.

'I knew you would...'

'Dad, look!' I explode and hold out my arms. His face crumbles. There's a fleeting look of concern, before disgust creeps over his features. His disdainful eyes, his screwed up nose and his frown all tell me that I repulse him. I hesitate. But his arms remain open. I go to him and he folds them around me.

'What is it, Ibiya?'

'I don't know.'

'When did...?'

'I just noticed it. It wasn't there earlier.'

'Moses! This is not acceptable. You are my son. He has gone too far...'

'Dad, let them go.' I plead. 'Just let the Israelites go. This is too much. I can't...' I run out of words to express myself.

He doesn't speak immediately. It seems like a long time before he forms his response. He considers it thoroughly first. 'No, Ibiya. I'm sorry.'

I close my eyes. I can't believe he just...

'We'll fix this. I'll make it go away, Ibiya. I simply won't let this happen to you.'

He sends for the magicians. He waits. I wait, incredulous. Hurt and confused, itching all over and feeling alone. The messenger returns alone. They won't come. They have this curse on them too. They're covered in boils. Black, flaky, sore boils and they're ashamed to face their Pharaoh.

'The priests then. Bring the priests.'

We wait again. I can't bring myself to look at Dad. He's trying so hard, but surely he knows by now that none of this will help. I just want so much for him to listen to me. Really listen and hear what I'm saying. It won't work. My heart aches. My father sees my pain and still refuses to do the one thing that is guaranteed to end it. Does he even care about me or am I just another weapon in his armoury? The messenger returns with his eyes averted and straining to keep a slight shake under control. It's bad news. He tentatively shakes his head and then flees before my father has a chance to react. He turns to me instead.

'I'm sorry... Ibiya, I...' His voice wobbles. I hear his sigh of frustration but I don't believe in it. I slowly walk away.

Chapter 22:

Umayma

Umayma was brooding and tired. Pili was at the table, jabbering away about today's happenings – what someone had said and done to somebody else and what they'd said back and who they'd told and... – but she wasn't really listening. She couldn't concentrate. She had her own concerns hanging over her, worries that she couldn't share with Pili. She was too young to be burdened with things neither of them could change. It wouldn't be fair. So Umayma kept it to herself. She pondered over and over again the crusty black mark she'd spotted on the back of her father's hand last night. How had it got there? And why had she been dismissed so hurriedly from the room? She'd stayed awake in bed listening to her mother's concerned tones and her father calmly trying to play things down. She hadn't slept much after that. It bothered her a lot that she was old enough to be left caring for the other two every day, but apparently not old enough to be told what was going on. It wasn't fair.

It didn't help that Sagira was fractious too. All morning Umayma had had to listen to her whinging.

Every time she'd put her down, she'd cried incessantly and pulled herself to her feet to try to toddle back to Umayma. Not being able to see clearly through her tears and puffy eyelids, she'd inevitably toppled over after the first step or two and hurt herself, making her cry even more. So Umayma had spent the entire morning with Sagira sitting either on her lap or her hip, which was compounding her exhaustion. There didn't seem to be anything actually wrong though. Umayma had checked. Sagira had no temperature. She'd slept well, eaten breakfast, she was clean and not teething, so Umayma was annoyed. Why, when she really needed an easy day, did she have a clingy, irritable toddler? Perhaps, she thought with a heavy sigh, her own mood had unsettled Sagira.

'You're not even listening to me, Umayma!' Pili yelled, thumping her hand down on the table.

'Sorry, Pili,' she replied wearily. 'What were you saying?'

'Haven't you heard anything I've said? My best friend in the world is not allowed out to play today. She's ill. And the others have been calling her horrible names. They won't even play with me either because they say I must have it too. I don't though, do I? So they shouldn't be saying...'

'Who's ill?'

Pili shoved the table in frustration. A jug of water wobbled violently. She reached out to grab it but the rim escaped her clutch and her fingers skimmed the outside, sending it further off balance. It toppled over. The earthenware clunked against the table and water flung itself over Sagira and Umayma. Sagira screamed.

'Look what you've...!' Umayma began without thinking, but a distraught Pili had already disappeared through the door.

With a sigh Umayma clambered to her feet and lifted Sagira onto the table. She spoke softly, trying to calm her enough to peel off the wet linen that clung to her skin. Supporting Sagira's unsteady weight beneath her arms, Umayma turned her slowly. Her hand flew to her mouth. She screamed, startling Sagira again. Sagira lost her balance and landed hard on the table, sending her into a new surge of shaking and shuddering. Umayma's own chest was heaving too as she struggled to keep her reaction under control for Sagira's sake. She hadn't meant to scare her. But the three large blackened patches of dry flaky skin on her back terrified her. She'd never seen anything like this. What was it? What was wrong with her baby sister? And what was she supposed to do?

'Pili!' She called. She held Sagira close and cuddled her on her shoulder, bobbing rhythmically up and down to comfort her. She grabbed the doll up from the floor and stroked it slowly against her sister's cheek. Sagira pushed it away. 'Pili, where are you? Please!' she implored. 'Please come back, Pili. I'm not cross. I need your help. Pili!' Umayma went outside and looked around. She ignored the horrified gasps and pointing fingers. She ignored the woman sternly telling her to 'get that child back inside at once.' She strained to see up to the roof. 'Pili, are you up there? Come down! I need you to ...' Pili wasn't there. Her voice faded to a whisper. 'Sagira's not well. She needs help.'

Umayma stood on the street, cuddling Sagira close. 'Please be well,' she whispered over and over again to her as she thought what to do. Where was Pili? She didn't know and she couldn't worry about that now. Sagira had to come first. She needed someone to fetch her mother from the granary and if Pili weren't here to do it, she'd have to go herself. She darted back into the house and grabbed a blanket to cover her sister's exposed back. She couldn't bear the staring any more. With a last hurried sweep of the street, she strode off to get help, her pounding feet sending clouds of dust up from the street.

Chapter 23:

A change of heart?

Moses stretched. He rubbed his temples. He shuffled. He took a deep breath and lifted his head to face Aaron again. He was rehearsing. And quickly losing his nerve.

'Thus says the Lord, the God of the Hebrews, "Let my people go, that they may serve me. For this time I will send all my plagues on you and your servants and your people, so that you may know that there is no one like me in all the earth."' He sighed. '"For if by now I had put forth my hand and struck you and your people with pestilence, you would then have been cut off from the earth. But, indeed, for this reason I have allowed you to remain, in order to show you my power and in order to proclaim my name through all the earth. Still you exalt yourself against my people by not letting them go."'

Aaron nodded. He patted Moses on the shoulder. Moses steadied himself. He was feeling scared, scared of facing Pharaoh again. Scared of what would happen if Pharaoh responded the way he expected him to, scared of where all this was heading. He did not like the effects his words were having on Egypt or on Israel. He was uncomfortable with his role.

The mood in Goshen was sombre. God was exempting them from the plagues themselves, now that the severity was escalating. But they were marked out. Different. Special. And that brought its own backlash. Things had always been hard for an Israelite in Egypt. Now it was becoming unbearable. Pharaoh hated them. Pharaoh's people hated them. They blamed them for this. Although they had done nothing except continue working as usual, harder than usual, they'd become Pharaoh's scapegoats. They were being paid back, every day, every hour, with harder work, harsher treatment and worse conditions. Being an Israelite had always carried a stigma. Now it was incomparably worse. There was no point moaning or being angry. And really, there was no one to be angry at. Some had directed their frustrations at Moses, but even they knew really that he was only a messenger. Most just quietly gritted their teeth and endured the daily onslaught.

Moses felt bad. He wanted this to end more than anyone. He had heard God's promise to release the people firsthand and he was more than ready to see it happen. To give them the better life that lay just out of reach. But it wasn't in his power. He couldn't do anything to speed this up. That was his personal burden.

All he could do was to carry on bringing the messages and enduring the pain. Hope was beginning to hurt.

He walked to the palace with his head low and his mind overflowing with thoughts. As much as he detested Pharaoh, Moses was intrigued by Ibiya. This boy had a heart. Moses had watched him handle those dying animals, transfixed. Ibiya had known that the creatures had been sentenced to death but he hadn't walked away. He'd paced. He'd chewed his thumbnails. He was certainly no expert shepherd. Despite that, he'd stayed out there, monitoring, doing all he could to diagnose and treat the problem to prevent it from escalating. He knew what he was doing was a lost cause. But that didn't stop him. His concern for the animals' welfare struck Moses deeply. He had not expected it. So young and yet so dedicated. Ibiya cared. Where did that come from? His father? Moses doubted it. He scoffed at the idea. He wondered if Dudimose even knew the torment his son had put himself through out there. He suspected not. Moses thought over his words again and sighed. He felt Aaron beside him like his shadow, silent but faithful. The mood was tense.

The men entered the courtyard. The routine was getting old. They waited. Pharaoh made them wait. When he arrived, he did not greet them. They did not expect a welcome. But today Moses noticed that Pharaoh seemed a little less hard somehow; less powerful and threatening. More humble. Was God's message finally getting through? Moses hoped so. He didn't dare get excited, but the thought that this might be the day Israel would leave made his heart jump. He reminded himself not to underestimate Pharaoh and began his prepared speech. He was firm but not overconfident. He was, after all this, tired of being the messenger. Why me? he thought again, as the rehearsed words practically spoke themselves. When he had given Pharaoh God's warning about his attitude and actions, Moses went into more specifics.

"'Behold, about this time tomorrow, I will send a very heavy hail, such has not been seen in Egypt from the day it was founded until now. Therefore, bring your livestock and whatever you have in the field to safety. Every man and beast that is found in the field and is not brought home, when the hail comes down on them, will die.'"

Moses left the palace courtyard having received no immediate response, wondering whether this would be the one that would change Pharaoh's heart. He would have loved to receive an immediate reaction. He had no choice now other than to wait for one.

Part four

Consequences

Chapter 24:

Control

'Get these cows inside!' I yell. I'm walking the land, inspecting the situation at the start of what's going to be a very tough day. My herd of cattle is still out in the field. I'd hoped that everything would be under shelter by now. An experienced farm worker in the next field looks up. He shakes his head and returns to his work. I smile. He can't have heard me properly.

Moses is sitting in the shade of a fig tree. Its wide, low branches provide plenty of cover and keep him cool. I shake my head and wipe the sweat from my forehead. I wish I could be so relaxed. Aaron has left. He's chosen to return to Goshen, but Moses has stayed, out of curiosity perhaps, or so I can't forget what he's just done. It doesn't matter. I don't have time to worry about it now.

I'm about to go over and repeat my instruction to the hardened farm worker when a younger boy approaches me. He is weighed down with equipment; yokes and heavy coils of rope.

'Excuse me,' he squeaks with an awkward bow. He seems nervous. 'I wouldn't waste your time. He won't do it.' I'm stunned.

'I'm sorry?' I'm feeling quite indignant and can't quite understand what this farm hand is trying to tell me. What does he mean, he won't do it? I'm being advised by someone no more than my own age who is at the bottom of the chain of command here. I know I'm young, but my status should speak for itself. And I've been given specific authority here. I'm irritated by this blatant lack of respect. I scowl.

'A message came from Pharaoh early this morning.' He bows again, trying to soften me. 'He instructed us to go about our business as usual today, in spite of anything Moses may do. He specifically said that we should not employ any special measures...' He trails off.

My hands have found their way onto my hips and I raise my voice so that my message will be heard by everyone nearby. I do not want to have to repeat myself. 'I am in authority here. The farmland is mine to manage. These animals are under specific threat while in the field and we need to move them to safety. Now, please.'

The boy looks at me. He looks at the farm worker, his superior, and back to me. I can tell he is torn. He drops the cumbersome equipment onto the ground and tentatively approaches a nearby cow. Patting it on the back to encourage it into motion, he speaks in gentle tones. I nod my approval. He avoids eye contact and moves slowly. Heaving a sigh, I make my way to the worker who is now shifting the flock onto fresh grass.

'These sheep need to be under shelter today.' I speak gently. I can't afford to be heavy-handed with someone who knows his job so well. He's worked these fields and tended these animals longer than I've been alive. But, I'm in charge now. 'I need you to take them in,' I say with all the firmness I can muster.

'With due respect, Ibiya,' he replies, 'the Pharaoh would like me to go about my business as usual. Until you wear the crown, it's his instructions I'll be following.' He nods and turns away.

'Do you realise that these creatures are the subject of the next curse?' He does not reply. 'Animals that you have bred, nurtured and cared for, for years, will be struck down today.' He weaves to one side of the meandering flock to keep them in line. 'You've already lost most of them to the disease. Do you really want to risk...? I may not know these creatures as you do, but I have their best interests at heart. I want to see them safe.'

'I can't do it, Ibiya.' He looks me in the eye. His own deep-brown pair is tinged with sadness and when he speaks, his voice is flat. 'I have to follow my instructions.'

I feel his struggle. I nod. It's futile trying to persuade him. He's been loyal to my dad all his life, and I'm asking him to go against that. He genuinely can't do it. He fears the consequences and he trusts my father with his life – and those of his animals – even in the face of such bizarre instructions.

I sigh and look round. Moses is still here. I watch him for a while. He's leaning on the trunk of the tree, enjoying the rest and taking in the tranquil scene. The tension of waiting is driving me mad. I'm stressed. I can't concentrate. I don't know when the hail is coming. And I'm not in control. I should at least be in control of my workers.

That's the one part I *can* potentially deal with. I stride off in the direction of the palace. I'm entering the grounds when a messenger approaches to update me. It seems that some of the farmers have listened to my advice. They have sheltered their animals. I realise what a brave decision that was for them. They're acting directly against Pharaoh. But the workers are split. Many still have animals out.

'Dad. What's going on?'

'Ibiya, when I asked you to keep me updated, I did not expect you to come personally. You should be in the fields now. We have messengers for...'

'Am I responsible for what's happening in our farms or not?' He looks confused.

'Yes son, of course. I placed you to oversee...'

'Then why do you insist on interfering?' He looks at me, clearly taken aback. I rub my temples and hold my ground.

'Ibiya, I do not know what you mean. Why this outburst?'

I narrow my eyes and feel my nostrils flaring. He's being difficult.

'I have farmers refusing to follow my direction because you have issued your own instructions. You are undermining...'

'Which instructions?'

'You have asked them to continue as normal. You don't want Moses to think...'

He chuckles. My face flushes. 'That was simply a piece of advice. I meant only to reassure my people that everything was under control. I did not want panic in my land. You do not yet have the authority and power to instil that sort of calm.'

'You can't keep out of it, can you? I do not yet have any authority because you will not let it go. Animals will die today... Most have already been killed off... If we do not take them in, we will lose what little labour and resources we have left from them. We will lose another source of food entirely. The feast for your grand temple opening will be pathetic without meat.'

'Go back out there and take control of the situation, Ibiya. I trust you. Do what it takes to protect our resources. I will have meat.'

'Dad, they won't listen. Their Pharaoh has told them to carry on as usual. They simply will not comply with any instructions I issue that go against that!' I look directly into his eyes. 'I need you to retract what you told them.'

'No.' His eyes have lost their glimmer.

'No?'

'Firstly, Pharaoh does not retract instructions. I do not change my mind with the wind. At all times, I am decisive and firm. Secondly, I really don't believe Moses should have the satisfaction of seeing our schedule thrown into disarray. He's out there today, isn't he? Watching to see what happens.'

'Yes, but...'

'I'm sorry, Ibiya. My answer is no.'

'I only want to take sensible precautions. Something will happen, like it did last time, and the time before. We can minimise the impact by...'

'That barley crop?'

'Yes?'

'You said it was ruined?'

'Yes.'

'Yolk up the cattle. I want every barley field ploughed and ready for re-planting. We need to optimise productivity now to make up the shortfall.'

'This is all a joke! I'm not actually managing anything, am I?'

'While you're in here moaning, instead of being out there leading, I have no choice but to assume control.'

My fists ball up. I'm tense and hot. As I slowly release them, my heart sinks. I'm angry, but it's not achieving anything, except to make me feel like a failure. Nothing I say will change anything. I will never win. He simply won't let me.

Chapter 25:

Seven

A bolt of flaming, golden light shot out of the heavens and sped through the air. For one tiny moment, the landscape was brightly illuminated before dusky shadows consumed the view again. Dudimose blinked. He could still see the shapes of the city against a brilliant white background imprinted in his vision. He'd never seen anything like it before. He looked around. He'd come to his podium alone to reflect on the day's events, but now he wished Ibiya was here. He stared out across Egypt, beautiful in this evening light, looking for signs of anything unusual. Everything seemed normal. He couldn't imagine what had caused such a sudden and bright fire in the sky. Or why it would disappear so fast. He was still feeling unnerved when a distant growl, growing rapidly louder and fiercer, assaulted his ears. It rumbled around in the sky. Dudimose scanned the view, searching for the source of the sound. He stepped back from the edge of the podium, feeling unsure. It didn't seem to belong to anything. Silence and stillness filled the space again, but Dudimose was rattled. He fought to control his shaky hands and breathed shallow breaths.

Before Dudimose's wide, terrified eyes, a second fiery streak tore the darkness in two. A second roll of thunder resounded, coming at him from all sides. Loud, savage blasts exploded above his head. He was paralysed with fear. Shifting and stirring in the sky, dark shadows billowed. A deafening crack echoed across Egypt and the onslaught began.

Dudimose stood motionless as the ground before him was struck with a succession of large raindrops. They shot towards him with the unnerving speed of arrows in battle and bounced hard off the steps. A chill ran through him. This was not like any rain he'd seen before. Each round droplet struck the ground and clattered noisily, drumming down the flight of steps. At the bottom, a growing mass of white beads blanketed the ground. Dudimose was transfixed. He could not tear his eyes away from the driving downpour. Faltering, he extended his open palm into the stream. Needle-sharp pain darted through his skin. His fingers turned red and his hand stung. Dudimose withdrew his arm and rubbed his hands together. He shivered. A chill had arrived with the fast-flowing wind and swept right through Dudimose. His skin was damp and covered in tiny pimples. He was cold. More than that, he felt an eerie sensation as though a warm flame somewhere deep inside of him had just been extinguished too. His heart froze. He felt hollow and dispassionate, strangely apathetic about Egypt and his own role. He was conscious enough of this happening to be unsettled, but not strong enough to resist the shift. It was as though someone else was in control now. That scared him. His bottom lip quivered.

Egypt lit up again as lightning forked to the ground in sharp, jagged spears. The rumble followed faster than before, and louder. Dudimose flinched. It had startled him. He sank to his knees on the podium and agonised over what had gone wrong. What had he done to deserve any of this? He felt his greatness slipping from his grasp and he sobbed. As the hail continued to drive down, Dudimose knelt weeping.

A hand landed firmly on his shoulder.

'Dad, get up.'

A messenger scurried away. Dudimose flushed red. He was embarrassed and that made him angry. He scrabbled to get to his feet. He looked over his shoulder. Concern oozed from Ibiya's face.

'Go inside. You can't stay here like this. You're cold and damp and...'

His son was worried about him. He had to be strong, get back in control. He must show Ibiya that he could handle himself and everything else that was... the thought made him weep again. Tears rolled down his cheeks. He hadn't cried for years, since he'd become Pharaoh, and now it felt like he would never be able to stop. He was relieved that in the darkness and hail it was unlikely that Ibiya could tell.

'Dad, you can't stay here. They'll see you. Nobody should see you like this. You can't let...'

Dudimose nodded slowly. His son was right. If he was seen like this, that would be the end. The physical and mental strength that he had run laps round the temple to demonstrate, the stamina he'd shown through his years of leadership, would be undermined in a second if... He peered through his tears and through the darkness. Was anyone out there? He doubted anyone would be that foolish, but Ibiya was right. He had to get inside. He staggered away from the steps. Ibiya did not follow. He stood at the top of the steps, head down, one arm covering his face. Was he preparing to...?

'Son?'

'You go inside, dad. I won't be long, I have to...' He was shouting to be heard above the thunder.

'Come now. I... Please.'

'Soon. I must check the fields. I think some animals were left out. They'll be terrified. I don't know what they'll...'

'No!' Dudimose commanded with all the strength he could muster. His voice was shaky and he couldn't be sure it hadn't been drowned out by the hail.

'Get inside, Dad. I'll be back before you know it.' He stretched his leg to take his first step into the elements, but Dudimose was faster. He crossed the podium and grabbed his firstborn by the wrist. He grasped hold with all his strength. He had no intention of letting go. Ibiya struggled. He twisted and yanked to free his hand. He pulled away. Dudimose twirled him by the shoulder to look him in the eyes.

'They're dead! If they aren't already they soon will be. Look out there! Look! They won't survive this. Nothing will.'

'I can get them inside. I can...'

'You won't survive out there. I will not let you go.'

'I'm not asking your permission anymore, Dad. I'm going. Perhaps Moses should just do the same! You can't keep controlling everything I...' He struggled free of Dudimose's hold.

'Because I love you, Ibiya.'

Ibiya hesitated. His foot was already on the top step, but he looked back, unsure.

'They've ruined so much. So much, but...'

Ibiya shook his head.

'But what, Dad?'

'I'll let the cattle die, Ibiya, yes. But not you.' His eyes were solemn and his voice was strong. He wanted his son to know how much he meant this; to see the heart beneath his facade. 'I will not lose you over this. I would never do that. Never.'

Ibiya rolled his eyes. 'Dad, I'll be careful. But I have to…'.

Dudimose grabbed his young son around the waist and hauled him back onto the podium. He stumbled. Sprawling, they fell to the ground. They landed heavily, awkwardly. Lightning flashed and thunder erupted simultaneously. The bluish-yellow light was blinding. It struck a statue within the palace courtyard and split it in two. The halves crashed to the ground and crumbled on impact. The image of Pharaoh lay smouldering in the driving hail.

Ibiya's face drained of colour. He was shaking. Dudimose cradled his son and let the tears flow.

Chapter 26:

Rasui

Rasui tore a corner off the remains of yesterday's bread and passed it on. He looked at the scrap in his hand. He was hungrier than this, but there were plenty more servants stranded here tonight and not nearly enough to feed them all. They'd watched ravenous as plate after plate of delicious food had been carried past them, up to the Pharaoh. Rasui's heart had sunk when their own meagre leftovers were brought in and a collective groan emanated from the crowd around him. The next boy took an unreasonably large chunk before passing it on. Rasui looked at him, one eyebrow raised.

'What?' He shot back. 'You could have taken more.' Rasui shook his head. It was going to be a long evening. He didn't want to get into an argument now. Crammed into a small room next to the palace kitchen, they were all off-duty. But as long as the lightning continued its indiscriminate strike, they were unable to leave the safety of the palace. The storm outside raged. None of them would dare to make the journey home in these conditions. Every now and then the dim room was illuminated as a bolt of lightning lit up the sky outside the window. The thunder rumbled through even the thick palace walls so that they could feel, more than hear, its sinister grumblings.

The conversation revolved endlessly around this extreme attack of weather and the previous six plagues. Rasui avoided eye contact. He wasn't in the mood for talking. What he'd seen on duty tonight had unnerved him more than anything Moses had inflicted. And he strongly suspected he was going to lose his job any minute now. He kept his head down and nibbled on the stale bread. He wished he could be home. He needed to know that everyone was safe. He hoped they were. Please let them all be safe, he mouthed silently. He hoped they'd realise that he was too. He knew his mother would be worrying, and Kepi too. He also knew that his father would have the sense to keep everyone calm. At least he hoped so.

Another nagging thought kept returning to Rasui too. Soon someone would realise. He'd be found out and then they'd come and humiliate him in front of these people. He'd lose his job. His heart was racing and he felt queasy. He was certain it wasn't the bread, however hard and stale it had been. He knew he'd let the Pharaoh down and he felt the full weight of guilt and responsibility. Why hadn't he found a way to deliver that message? He felt stupid and inadequate and hollow inside. How could he break the news to his family? He'd let them down badly too. When they dismissed him, would he have to leave immediately, in this storm? He probably deserved to be sent out there to die. He shuddered. His face was pale. He put his arms around his groaning stomach and let his head drop onto his knees. He could have made a difference tonight, couldn't he?

Rasui wasn't able to shift the image of Pharaoh weeping at the top of those steps from his mind. He'd arrived there with a message from the farm workers to find Pharaoh alone and contemplatively staring out across Egypt. He was supposed to tell Pharaoh that they'd seen the storm coming on the horizon and realised its extreme severity. They believed Moses' words and wanted to save the animals by moving them to shelter as Ibiya had instructed, but needed Pharaoh's approval. Rasui was meant to ask for the approval and return immediately with an answer. Speed was critical. But something about Pharaoh's pensive stance had made Rasui reluctant to interrupt. Pharaoh had not heard him approach. He'd gently cleared his throat but that had gone unnoticed too. Then Rasui had stood excruciatingly dithering on the spot, waiting to be invited to speak, unsure whether to announce himself or not. He had a sense in his gut that if he interrupted Pharaoh now, it would anger him. Rasui had no desire to be on the receiving end of Pharaoh's anger. But he was also scared to leave without an answer. He'd felt ripped in two by his indecision. He'd concentrated hard on blending into the shadows and reluctantly watched Pharaoh's apparent breakdown unfold until Ibiya had arrived and given him the opportunity to flee unnoticed. Now he could only wait until his transgression was discovered.

Huddled in that palace storeroom, Rasui was a wreck. He was concerned for himself and his family if he lost his job tonight. Worse than that was the horrible secret he carried. While others worried aloud about the effects of the hail and what Moses might do next, Rasui worried that Egypt would flounder and drown like a wildcat in the Nile under this sustained attack, unless it had strong leadership. The future looked bleak. Pharaoh was a mess. If he couldn't fight this, how could his people? Surely if Pharaoh was so intimidated, the rest of Egypt should be too. Rasui couldn't help wondering what Pharaoh knew, that he hadn't shared with his people.

Chapter 27:

Death and destruction

'I've sent for Moses, Ibiya.' My father's voice is weak and his eyes betray his pain. He's humble after our argument, coming to find me in a first move I certainly hadn't expected from him. 'I've been unfair on you. Expecting so much... making it so hard.' Tears start to well up in his eyes again. I shake my head.

'It's... This isn't your fault.

'That's sweet, Ibiya, but it's not true. You know I've handled this badly,' he coughs, 'and I haven't been listening to you.'

I don't know how to respond. I look away, feeling uncomfortable with this new, soft side to my father. I'm unsure whether I should even believe it. It seems genuine, but... I wrap my arms across my chest. I want to be able to trust my dad. He's right though. He hasn't been fair. I'm filled with a strange mix of relief that he's realised my feelings, and anger that it's taken so long. I look at him sideways.

'Do you think the damage will be bad?' He asks meekly. I nod slowly. It's going to be horrendous. My animals and crops will not have withstood the pounding hail and random strikes of fire. Dad saved me. But he didn't let me save them. I close my eyes. I don't even want to imagine what I'll find when I go out to the land again.

We walk to the court together. Today Dad is not making anyone wait. He'll be in position, ready to start proceedings as soon as Moses and Aaron have battled their way through the hail. As we stand side by side on the marble floor, framed by pillars, I begin to feel that we're working together again. We've disagreed for so long and yet, now Dad is acting more reasonably, I find myself forgiving him without really choosing to. It's just happening automatically. I'd expected that my anger would still be in the way. And I am still cross but I'm willing to support him too. He's proved that I come first.

Moses and Aaron arrive. They walk across the court until they face us, dripping wet and bedraggled and looking surprised to see us already there. I look at Dad. He does not waste any time. His face is more human today, more like the person I usually see away from the public, and his voice is less controlled, less harsh. Is this for show or has he really changed?

'I have sinned this time; the Lord is the righteous one, and I and my people are the wicked ones. Make supplication to the Lord, for there has been enough of God's thunder and hail; and I will let you go, and you shall stay no longer.'

I'm impressed. That was clear and to the point. He has not toyed with them or imposed his superiority. He's spoken to them as equals. Perhaps this experience really has changed him. Moses is less convinced. It's clear on his unmoved features. I can't blame him. All the evidence certainly suggests this is too good to be true. Moses probably suspects another act, but I've seen this change of behaviour in private too. I don't think this is a show.

'As soon as I go out of the city, I will spread out my hands to the Lord;' he says. His voice is level, unemotional. He seems a little detached. 'The thunder will cease and there will be hail no longer, that you may know that the earth is the Lord's.' Now he looks at my father and a little life returns to his words. 'But as for you and your servants, I know that you do not yet fear the Lord God.'

'Why would he say that?' I ask, as Moses follows Aaron out of the court. 'I think it's obvious you have changed your mind. I think it took a while for them to convince you, but the hail...' I trail off, noticing dad's frown.

'I should have brought the animals under shelter. He's right. They warned me. I just didn't think it was... I'm sorry, Ibiya.'

'You've done the right thing, letting them go. I know that was hard for you to do, but I really think it's best for Egypt. We can't keep on...' I stop myself again. Dad is feeling sensitive today. Perhaps it's because he came so close to losing me. 'Come with me. I'll show you why.'

We walk out to the podium. I'm halfway down the steps when I realise that Dad is not following me. He's looking out across Egypt with a sorrowful gaze. The hail and thunder has stopped. The sky is blue again. Moses has been faithful to his word. But the ground is still covered in a layer of white that clearly shows up the devastation. In the courtyard, the fallen statue lies in cracked and shattered pieces. The surfaces are dimpled all over from the continual pounding of the hail. Beyond the gates, more structures have fallen or been struck and split, scorched, cracked, weathered and battered. Bodies lie in the streets. People who decided to brave the elements, for what? I sigh, realising how close I'd come to being one of them.

'Ibiya, I can't go out there.'

'Dad, you need to see this. You need to understand why you're doing the right thing, and then you won't feel tempted to change your mind again. You have to see what their God is capable...'

'This view represented beauty and strength.'

'Yes, I...'

'It makes me angry, Ibiya. I'm angry.'

'I know, Dad. Come and see what...'

He follows me down the steps and across the courtyard. I stop to listen to a messenger.

'Ibiya,' he says. 'The new barley is utterly destroyed, and the flax. Many of the trees were struck and burned or split in two. It's chaos.'

'Did any of the animals sur...?'

He shakes his head. 'Only the few that were taken in. The rest are a mess. Their bodies are torn apart and mangled. I've never seen anything so...' His cheeks flush pink. 'I vomited. I couldn't bear the sight.' He takes my arm and leads me a few steps, glancing back over his shoulder at Dad. 'Most didn't take their animals in because Pharaoh instructed them not to. They have willingly followed his commands until now, but... they're losing patience. This was too much. The people are angry with Pharaoh. They don't understand why he doesn't end this.'

He's expecting a response but the only one I'm ready to give is 'Thank you. You may go.'

I turn back to find that Dad has gone. I drag my feet back up the steps to meet him on his podium. The people seem to want me to make some response of my own. I don't know whether they expect me to overrule my father. I'm feeling the weight of responsibility and I know he must be too. I have to support him through this. We have to get the people to believe in him again.

'Dad, let's go and meet the people. They need you to be among them now.'

'No, Ibiya. They need to see that I'm still strong. I need to repair and rebuild Egypt.' Glad to see a glimmer of passion return, I offer my support.

'What can I do to help?'

'Do what you can with the remaining crops.'

'Dad, no. I'm not accepting responsibility for farming any more. You said yourself, you've worked against me. I've got nothing left there.'

'You asked what you could do to help. You can't just abandon your workers after the worst crisis they've ever experienced!' I drag my hand across my forehead, exasperated.

'What will you do?'

'Start rebuilding. But I'm going to need my slaves.'

I drop my hands and stare. What can he be thinking? My father has just been consumed by foolishness and guided by evil. I feel my knees buckling beneath me. Everything blurs into darkness.

Chapter 28:

Insubordination

Moses had not expected any better from Pharaoh. He'd been extremely dubious about the latest offer to release the Israelites, especially as he'd still not shown any signs of listening to the warnings. Yes, he responded after the hail but, by now, Moses thought, surely Pharaoh understood that whatever God promised, he would deliver. This man, great ruler of Egypt, could surely not be ignorant of that. He must understand that he needed to respond. He could have saved the livestock and the portion of his population that hadn't had the sense to stay inside. He could have spared the crops. But no, Moses had seen instead how he'd risked his civilisation for the sake of his own personal pride. He'd known that Pharaoh was not yet ready to listen. He'd not actually believed they'd be going anywhere just yet. It was just as well he was sceptical. He wasn't sure he could take any more disappointment.

He thought about what God had said to him that morning as he'd strolled through Goshen, praying for breakthrough for his people. It certainly explained a few things about Pharaoh's behaviour. God had told him that he'd hardened Pharaoh's heart so that he could perform these signs. Without that information it all made no sense at all. Who could be this resistant, even if he did rule the great civilisation of Egypt? Now the extreme stubbornness made sense. But the rest of it had intrigued Moses too. Previously, God had always seemed to say that he wanted Pharaoh to see that he was Lord over all the earth. Now, he had said he wanted Israel to know; that he should tell his son and grandson the story of what was happening here, his signs, and his mockery of Egypt. Moses had mixed emotions about all that. It didn't seem at the moment that he'd ever be in another place looking back on all this to relate it to anybody. It felt like Pharaoh would go on being stubborn for ever and that God would go on showing everyone his character for ever. He could see no way out of this cycle. It seemed harsh to Moses that God wanted to mock Pharaoh though. Couldn't he just demonstrate his power by getting Israel out of this miserable predicament, out of this stupid unending battle of wills? Pharaoh had done a pretty good job of making himself look foolish without God's help. Why did he need to stress that even more?

Moses stood in Pharaoh's court waiting to announce plague eight. Eight chances! This was getting ridiculous. It seemed too generous. But if God really had hardened

Pharaoh's heart then it wasn't hard to predict what the outcome was going to be today. Being here felt futile.

Pharaoh had arrived. Moses sighed before he began. His eyes were pleading. He noticed Ibiya hang his head. Poor child. He'd got caught up in all this and didn't seem to know where he stood. Ibiya seemed to Moses to symbolise all the helpless lives that were unwittingly involved in this, on both sides of the impasse.

'Thus says the Lord, the God of the Hebrews, "How long will you refuse to humble yourself before me?"' A strange question coming from someone exacerbating the problem, thought Moses. You've hardened his heart – of course he'll refuse. '"Let my people go that they may serve me. For if you refuse to let my people go, behold, tomorrow I will bring locusts into your territory. They shall cover the surface of the land, so that no one will be able to see the land. They will also eat the rest of what has escaped – what is left to you from the hail – and they will eat every tree which sprouts for you out of the field. Then your houses shall be filled, and the houses of all your servants, and the houses of all the Egyptians, something which neither your fathers nor your grandfathers have seen, from the day that they came upon this earth, until this day."' How can he ignore the threat of certain starvation? Moses asked himself, and yet his heart sank deep with the expectation that that was exactly what Pharaoh was about to do. He turned and walked out of the court with Aaron.

As they left the hall, Moses heard raised voices from inside. People seemed to be addressing Pharaoh in protest, pleading with him.

'How long will this man be a snare to us?' It's not my fault, Moses thought indignantly. The ruckus grew louder as more and more joined in.

'Let the men go, that they may serve the Lord their God.' Quite right, Moses nodded his unseen agreement. But, he pondered, there hadn't been anyone there except the servants. Were Pharaoh's own servants now turning against him too? How would he deal with that? Just as harshly as he'd treated the rest of the Egyptians, he predicted. He looked at Aaron, who seemed horrified at the uncharacteristic outburst within the palace.

'Do you not realise that Egypt is destroyed?'

Moses and Aaron hurried on as they heard footsteps approaching – neither wanted to be found listening in. But the messenger caught up with them anyway. They were summoned back to the court. Moses was confused. Had this mutinous uprising really had an impact?

Pharaoh was riled. His eyes were narrowed and his lips pursed in an expression of hatred. Veins in his neck were visibly throbbing. He was under great stress and looked to be close to rage.

'Go; serve the Lord your God! Who are the ones that are going?'

Moses took a deep breath. He didn't want to anger Pharaoh, but there was no way to lessen the impact he knew he was about to deliver. He spoke softly, but firmly.

'We shall go with our young and our old; with our sons and our daughters, with our flocks and herds we shall go, for we must hold a feast to the Lord.'

'Thus may the Lord be with you, if ever I let you and your little ones go!' Pharaoh exploded. 'Take heed, for evil is in your mind. Not so! Go now, the men among you, and serve the Lord, for that is what you desire.'

Moses and Aaron were swiftly escorted out from the court. As he left the palace grounds, Moses stretched out his staff and a wind began to blow over Egypt from the East.

Chapter 29:

Eight

The warm wind blows in my face. The linen fabric of my kilt ripples round my knees. It's a beautiful morning. I sigh. I'm standing in the centre of what used to be a field of flax. The hail has left it utterly devastated. I'm surrounded by jagged, broken stalks, most of which are bent double or lie flattened. The leaves are torn; shredded to pieces. And there are large, bare, blackened patches where lightening struck, surrounded by brown, scorched and withered leaves. I shake my head. It's such a waste. We've lost almost three quarters of our livestock to either the strange disease or the lightning and hail storm. The barley and flax are destroyed beyond any hope of rescue. Many of the trees have also been affected. And now we're expecting locusts. Moses explained in detail how they would destroy everything that remained. I look across to the fields of wheat and spelt which have not yet ripened. They managed to survive the hail, battered but relatively unscathed. They'll soon be gone along with all our fruit. How does Dad plan to feed everyone? The grain in stores won't last long.

I amble through the field, kicking a path through the fragile stalks, and think more about Dad. He has changed from being utterly broken, briefly repentant and humble, to being an absolute tyrant. I am convinced that he was determined to do the right thing. He was finally learning from his mistakes. He was beginning to appease his nation and end this catastrophic bombardment. And then... what happened? That question has been plaguing me ever since. Something did. Something, in the blink of an eye, caused a stark change. I can't deny it. Dad is rejecting all sense in favour of a belligerence which goes beyond even the worst of behaviour he'd displayed until now. Yes, he was stubborn; he was arrogant; he was blind to what he was facing – but not like this. He's ill; delusional or something. I won't be able to get him to a temple. He's refusing to leave the palace at all now. He's cut himself off from his people completely. But I have to do...

My thoughts are cut off. A dark cloud gathering on the horizon has gripped my attention. It's wide, extending as far as I can see in both directions, and tall. And it seems to be growing as I watch. Is this it? Are these the locusts that are going to destroy everything we have left? I don't have a chance to wonder for long. The cloud is moving towards me at immense speed. Dark-winged flecks like tiny birds shoot through the air. They dart and dive at random. The air is filled with chaotic movement. Within seconds they've covered the distance and they're approaching my face. I drop to the ground. It's dusty, hard and uncomfortable but I don't care. It's the safest place for me. Face down with arms shielding my eyes, I curl up and wait. How long before they pass over? They're moving fast, so it can't take that long even if the swarm is quite big. I lie, listening to the erratic buzzing. It's loud and close and the hum makes me feel drowsy.

My limbs stiffen. A locust has landed on my spine. I can feel its tiny legs distinctly as if my senses are heightened. I'm extremely aware of this creature on my back. It doesn't move. I don't move. Go on. Fly. It doesn't. As I remain frozen, willing the insect off me, my heart beating hard, the sound of the swarm changes. The drone of the beating wings is still there, but there's another sound; closer. It's right beside my ears and very different. It's a cutting, tearing sound. It surrounds me. I tilt my head up slowly until my eyes are just peeping out above my arm. In the narrow strip of vision between my arm and my eyelids, a dry, brownish body clings to the jagged green stem of flax. Four thin, angular legs support a stumpy, ridged body, which is part covered with smooth flat wings. An oval-shaped head propped up by two forelegs probes the crop with its long, curved, black antennae. Its eyes make my stomach churn. I feel sick. They are disproportionately large and striped the same earthy brown as the rest of its body. Brown ridges run down its face to an odd flap that covers its mouth. The mouth is surrounded by odd feelers that move across the surface of the flax as it flexes its head forward and back. My eyes widen as I watch the speed at which it munches through its meal. Large chunks disappear, one after the other in systematic curves around the body. It works so fast that it simply strips the plant back and forth, adjusting the position of its forelegs to maintain balance. I raise my head slightly further to see more. Hundreds of the insects are crowded into the small patch of land in front of me. Several to a stem, they eat as if there is no tomorrow. It's terrifying. I feel sweat pooling in the palms of my hands and running down my forehead and cheeks. On the ground, many more hop around in search of a feeding patch that has not already been claimed. Their hopping is as erratic as their flight. Each sudden leap propels them high into the air and far forward. They have no regard to what they land on. I am now covered. Locusts spring on my back, my head, my arms and legs. My skin is crawling. I itch all over. They sit on me, watching for their opportunity. Some launch themselves back into flight. They disappear from sight in a blink and join the dust cloud that blows over my head, moving faster than any other creature I know. I breathe short, shallow breaths, bury my head and wait for their destruction to be complete.

Chapter 30:

Khaldun

Miw-Sher curled up in a sunny spot in the middle of the garden. Her black-striped tail was curled around her and one paw covered her face. Khaldun was pulling up plants nearby. He longed to reach out and pick up Miw-Sher. He wanted to cuddle and stroke her like he used to, but she hadn't yet forgiven him since the gnat bites. He couldn't get near her without her claws coming out and her back arching, so he had to be satisfied with watching her. He sighed. It hurt to give her the space she was demanding – it seemed unnatural when they'd been so inseparable – but he hoped that, if he did, she'd soften to him again eventually.

Tearing his eyes painfully away from Miw-Sher, Khaldun pulled up another battered and torn plant. He was trying to deal with the storm damage. He was working his way across the plot, removing anything that had been destroyed by the hail or lightning. His personal plot of land was generous, larger than most of the other houses bothered with, and they had servants tending it for them. His family could have too, if they wanted. But it was another one of his father's ideas to keep him occupied with something beneficial. He remembered staring at the bare square of ground in dismay when his father presented him with the 'gift'. He hadn't wanted it to begin with. He couldn't think of anything worse than getting his hands dirty and spending hours on his knees in the heat. Today he'd stood looking at the plot, feeling that same dismay all over again. This time because the results of all his hours of careful planning, planting and nurturing had been destroyed overnight. Life was so unjust.

Sweat dripped from Khaldun's face and his throat was scratchy with thirst, but he wasn't going to stop just yet. There was only one corner left to rescue and he was determined to recover as much as he could. He was taking out his anger as he worked. Removing the evidence of destruction was his personal revenge on the storm. This garden would look good again. A sizeable heap was forming on the path where Khaldun was slinging any plants that were beyond help. It represented the large majority of his garden. There were, however, a small number of plants that had escaped well enough to be replanted, staked, supported and watered, which Khaldun believed would survive and, given sufficient time and attention, potentially thrive.

Finally, Khaldun clambered to his feet, stretched out and surveyed his work. He felt a pang of loss as he examined the bare expanse of earth. He forced himself to focus on the survivors and fabricated a belief in himself that he was capable of turning this disaster around. He wasn't convinced yet, but he'd try. With that thought he went into the house to wash and refresh himself. He called Miw-Sher, but with a disdainful look, she remained behind. Khaldun sighed. He missed her company.

He took a long refreshing gulp from his cup and wandered over to the window. He put the cup to his lips again and enjoyed the cool water. As he finally satisfied his thirst and lowered the cup, he blinked. An odd haze obscured his view of the garden. Khaldun stared harder. He couldn't make out much in the frenzied movement. Hundreds and thousands of large insect-like creatures were swarming above his garden. Some kind of creature had invaded. He'd never seen anything like this before. Everything was blurred but he could tell that the insects were much larger than either the gnats or flies had been. And yet, whatever this was, there seemed to be just as many. A constant buzz circled around in his head. The tone changed as the oversized insects dived to the ground and settled on both the abandoned heap of plant waste and the survivors, barely clinging onto life. He felt his indignation rise and anger flood through him, and another terrifying thought occurred to him. Where was Miw-sher? Was she still outside? He peered hard through the murky cloud. It was difficult to distinguish anything from here. His poor cat. She'd be traumatised all over again. He hurried through the maze of rooms and out to the garden. He covered his face with one arm and ran along the path.

'Miw-Sher!' His body was struck with needle sharp pain as the insects flew into him at top speed and ricocheted off the ground. He glimpsed his African wildcat sitting amongst the plants, one paw held aloft, batting the creatures away. They kept coming at her. He staggered over, one hand still protecting his eyes and scooped her up round her middle. He was about to carry her inside to relative safety when he noticed that his plants were being totally ravaged. He stopped in his tracks, emotion welling up inside him. Miw-Sher struggled. Khaldun stared in disbelief at the efficiency of the destruction. He forgot his own pain. He forgot Miw-Sher. He just stood and stared. Locusts continued to pound the skin of his arms and legs and Miw-Sher swiped his chest with her open claws before leaping down and slinking away into the shadows. Khaldun screeched in pain and retreated to the house.

Chapter 31:

Nine

Dudimose's footsteps padded softly. He walked slowly through the colonnade. It was still early. He hadn't been able to sleep so he'd eventually stopped trying and got up. He'd been walking for a while. He wasn't sure exactly how long, but it was still dark. Dudimose wasn't going anywhere in particular; he just found that walking took his mind off all the stresses that had been a constant presence over the last few days. Whenever he stopped to sit down or rest, his mind would flood with images of the horrors he'd inflicted on his nation. He knew it was all his fault. He knew he'd managed it badly. The guilt was almost too much to bear. Instead of protecting his people, he'd led them deeper and deeper into this nightmare. He shuddered again now. He stretched out a hand to feel the position of the last column and kept it there as he turned the corner. He walked on, letting his hand fall to his side and counting his steps.

Dudimose sighed. For no particular reason he stopped walking. He was tired. He couldn't carry on pacing for ever. It made him feel like a crazy person.

Perhaps he was though, he thought to himself. That would explain his behaviour with Moses yesterday. He'd wanted to let them go. He'd tried so hard. He'd admitted his sin against God and Moses. But then, somehow, against his own judgement, once the locusts had been driven to the red sea... what was wrong with him? He wasn't in control of himself anymore. How could he control a civilisation when he couldn't even keep his own words and actions under control? A tear rolled down his cheek. He shivered. What must Ibiya be thinking of him? Of all the people he'd let down, his son was the one that hurt the most. He'd set out to be such a good example; a role model for Ibiya to aspire to. He had planned to teach him so many good things about leadership. But what had he learned? Dudimose turned round, then back again. He needed to move. He couldn't bear this torment. But he couldn't decide which way to go. Everyone else was still sleeping and he didn't want to disturb them. They'd only tell him to sleep. They didn't understand. No one could.

Concentrate on work, concentrate on work, he told himself. The temple. Yes, my beautiful temple. Dudimose smiled. He was proud of the temple design and pleased with the progress that had been made in spite of all the setbacks. It was almost complete now and he was looking forward to publicly opening it. He'd have the opportunity to show his people that he was still the best Pharaoh Egypt had ever seen. They'd see that he'd been justified in keeping those Israelites here. He'd needed them, and all the trouble was worthwhile.

Military? Well, he'd ignored that situation for a while, but they'd looked after themselves well enough and nothing much had presented itself for them. Perhaps that could be Ibiya's new project. He had said that he was fed up with farming given everything that had happened recently. He'd like a new challenge; one that Moses couldn't interfere with and it might help to mend their friendship. Ibiya had been a bit distant lately. He kept looking at Dudimose oddly, like he had something contagious. Peculiar really, since Ibiya was the one with all the scarring from those ugly boils. Yes, he would let Ibiya take charge on that front. It'd cheer him up.

Dudimose didn't even want to think about the outlook for farming. A huge proportion of his population made their living on the land and he'd robbed them of that. He quickly shrugged off the self-condemnation and resolved that he'd get a trade solution established in the morning.

That only left the priests. He must meet with them too. He needed to instigate some extra special ceremonies. They could process in the temples bearing the images of the gods in their barques. They'd spare no trouble. This was going to be the last attempt to appease the gods and get them back on his side. Everything he'd tried so far had failed. They were simply not protecting Egypt and that had to change. Ibiya had suggested they might not be a match for Israel's god, but Dudimose knew that was nonsense. In all the confusion, he must have simply overlooked something. It was inexcusable, but whatever it was, was done now. He couldn't undo it. He could only seek to make things right again as soon as possible. And that's exactly what he planned to pour all his energy into. It'd take his mind off Moses, which was exactly what he needed. It'd be good for him.

Dudimose wondered whether it was almost sunrise yet. He thought it must be. He'd been up quite a while now going over his plan for the day. He turned and counted his steps along the colonnade, then carefully felt his way up the stairs to the corridor and then the podium. It was a shame that the hail had damaged so much of the view, but he would soon have it restored. His falcon was miraculously intact. There was at least one god out there he hadn't offended. He smiled to himself, looking forward to the sunrise and the perfect moment when the falcon would be cast into silhouette. Everything is going to work out well, he told himself.

Dudimose stood on his podium and waited for sunrise. He waited. He paced back and forth. He shuffled. He waited. There was no sign of the sky lightening at all. Perhaps he'd been awake earlier than he thought. After a while, Dudimose began to question his sanity. It was still perfectly dark out there and he was beginning to feel cold. Eventually he turned and felt his way tentatively back down the stairs towards the private part of the palace. He'd try to get some sleep until morning.

Chapter 32:

Dark times

I'm in bed. Still. I'm not sure anymore how long I've been here, lying still, unable to do anything. My stomach growls with hunger. I clutch one arm around it to try to lessen the pang I'm feeling. I roll over with a sigh. Time seems endless. This is the strangest thing I've experienced in my life. And the most agonising. It's dark. It's eerily quiet. And I'm so disorientated I have no idea how long I've been lying here. Days probably. My stomach is telling me it's too long. I'm hungry and restless. I can't get comfortable. I just turn over and over, trying to force my body to relax.

The air is thick and dank. It's hard to breathe, so my lungs work much faster than usual. Lying in the oppressive silence I'm painfully aware of my short shallow breaths. The air doesn't seem to get past my throat. My chest feels tight. I feel lightheaded. Dizzy. And I'm cold, so cold. I need to move around. Even curled up with the sheet tucked around me I can't get warm. I rub my limbs furiously, but it just takes my breath away. I shiver again.

I try to get up but the thick darkness is impenetrable. After lying for so long, I wobble. My legs feel numb and don't support my weight properly. I stumble around, bumping into things. I can't find the door. I can't even work out where I am in relation to anything. My breathing rate increases even more. I panic. So I stand still, trying to get my balance, looking around through the blackness for a glimpse of something to focus on. There's nothing, only thick, thick blackness. I sway slightly and steady myself. My own room has become some sort of cruel maze. I turn, lose my balance and fall over. My leg is going to have a bruise now. But I'd been standing up straight. How can I be so unaware of what's upright and what's not? It'd felt like I was stable, but apparently not. I don't like my sudden inability to control my body. It's disconcerting. I decide to get back into bed. At least then I'll know where I am. It'll be safer. And morning must be coming soon. It has to be. I pivot in circles on my hands and knees. I reach a hand out through the cold empty void. I can't get my bearings. I don't know where anything is. And my mind is playing strange tricks on me. I try to retrace my steps. I'm fairly certain my bed is in front of me. I edge slowly forwards, reaching out and fumbling round. But there's nothing. It can't have been this far away. Where is it? I pull myself a little further along, but my hand still swipes through nothingness. I turn, trying to keep track of how far. I hope I'm doubling back on myself. Taking a deep breath, I crawl again, slowly. I count my movements. After five I've found nothing. And still nothing after ten. This is not funny. I'm lost in my own room. I place my hands down one after the other and bring my knees forward several more times. Where am I? With more determination than I knew I was capable of, I decide this darkness is not going to beat me.

A wall! Good. That's good. I feel relieved that at least I have something solid as a reference point. I follow it along with my left hand, walking on my knees. They sting under the pressure, but I don't want to stand up in case I fall again. I don't know what's wrong with my balance. I feel so light-headed. I reach a corner and follow it round to the right. There must be something soon. I feel nervous as I make my way forward. Without being able to see, everything feels so unfamiliar, so hostile. I'm sure I've gone too far. This wall isn't usually this long. Should I go back? No, there's nothing there. Keep going, I tell myself. I think of the bed and the soft sheet and try to imagine myself lying enfolded in its warmth. It encourages me. I splay my fingers out and drag them along on the plaster surface of the wall. It's smooth and cold. Everything is cold. Without sunlight, all the warmth has disappeared. Suddenly my fingers lose contact with the wall. They flounder momentarily in the empty space where the wall should be. My arm drops to my side before I can react. I shuffle back and reach out my arm. There it is. I pat the surface to reassure myself. Slowly tracing it with my fingertips, I realise what was wrong. The wall turned a corner here – to the left. That's not right. I'm in my room. It's square. All the corners turn in. It doesn't open out like this. A cold sweat breaks out on my neck and back. I shiver. I'm more lost than I thought. I turn, putting my right hand to the wall now instead and pull myself to my feet. I must work this out. I must. How can I be somewhere I know so well and yet feel so adrift?

I can't work it out. Where am I? Tired, cold and damp, and without the strength to hope any more, I pull my knees to my chest and drop my head onto them. My shoulders heave. I shiver. I shudder and sob. I've never felt more afraid or alone.

Chapter 33:

The final confrontation

'Go, serve the Lord; only let your flocks and your herds be detained. Even your little ones may go with you.'

'You must also let us have sacrifices and burnt offerings, that we may sacrifice them to the Lord our God. Therefore, our livestock too shall go with us; not a hoof shall be left behind, for we shall take some of them to serve the Lord our God. And until we arrive there, we ourselves do not know with what we will serve the Lord.'

Moses held his ground. He'd heard enough of Pharaoh's empty promises, compromises and deals. When would he realise that God was not going to negotiate terms? He wanted his people out of Egypt, his way, on his terms, and – as Moses knew only too well – in his time. Moses would have loved to have got to the resolution much sooner, but God had this plan about first showing Pharaoh and then showing Israel his character. His power, yes, certainly they'd seen that. But Moses had been learning too that God did not force himself on Pharaoh. Time and time again he'd agreed to stop a plague only to be let down, but it didn't seem to stop him giving Pharaoh the next chance. There were consequences; gradually more serious and significant but each time an opportunity to do the right thing. Moses had had enough of delivering these messages, only to be mocked by Pharaoh. He had a strange feeling that God was losing patience too. Moses waited. He knew what Pharaoh was going to say because God had hardened his heart. He also felt instinctively that these were going to be Pharaoh's last words on the subject. God was going to have the final word. And soon.

Pharaoh stood silently contemplating Moses. Moses waited.

'Get away from me!' Pharaoh exploded. His rage was evident. All pretence at decorum and control was gone. His anger burned through his features, making them grotesque and ugly. His temples pulsed and his neck turned red. 'Beware; do not see my face again, for in the day you see my face you shall die!'

Moses watched Pharaoh hissing and spitting and pointing his finger, but he felt calm. The nerves he'd felt when he'd first addressed Pharaoh were gone. He'd felt small and unworthy in front of the King of Egypt then, now he felt pity for this shadow of a man, eaten away by his own stubborn pride. Though he was being subjected to a vicious verbal attack, he felt peaceful. This was out of his hands. He was only a messenger in this. He'd played his part – almost.

'You are right. I shall never see your face again!' Moses walked calmly out to the palace courtyard. Pharaoh followed. Moses looked at the gate, then he turned and went up the steps to Pharaoh's podium. Immediately several servants started scurrying around, whispering to each other, unsure whether they should stop him. Pharaoh narrowed his eyes, but did not move to prevent this insult. Moses addressed the small crowd of disgruntled workers milling around in the courtyard.

'Thus says the Lord, "About midnight I am going out into the midst of Egypt."' The crowd quietened and many turned to listen. Moses paused for the shushing and nudging to subside. '"And all the firstborn in the land of Egypt shall die, from the firstborn of Pharaoh who sits on his throne,"' there was an audible gasp, '"to the firstborn of the slave girl who is behind the millstones; all the firstborn of the cattle as well."' Animated whispers were passing through the growing crowd as pale-faced women confirmed with each other that they'd heard Moses correctly. '"Moreover, there shall be a great cry in all the Land of Egypt, such as there has not been before and such as shall never be again."' Pharaoh stood tall, stoically listening to the speech. It was impossible to know what he was thinking. '"But against the sons of Israel a dog will not even bark, whether against man or beast, that you may understand how the Lord makes a distinction between Egypt and Israel."' He looked at Pharaoh. 'All these your servants will come down to me and bow themselves before me, saying, "Go out, you and all the people who follow you," and after that I will go out.' Moses felt a flush of anger towards Pharaoh. He was suddenly hot and a surge of energy flooded through him. He looked at the faces of the Egyptians which showed every emotion from fear to relief, from admiration to hatred. Some simply looked stunned. Pharaoh had done this – to his own people. Moses had to get out of here. He was in a temper and didn't know what he may do if he looked at that man a moment longer. He'd murdered before and he knew what rage could do to a man. He stormed down the steps and through the gate.

He stomped through the streets of Egypt, past the enormous statue of Pharaoh, and towards the place where the frogs had been left to rot. Halfway there, he stood aside to let a procession pass. His heart was racing and the veins in his neck still throbbed. Priests carried a wooden barque supported by tall poles on their shoulders. It supported the golden image of one of Egypt's many gods. The model boat was exquisite in every detail, built to perfection and ornately decorated. Moses seethed. They walked reverently, surrounded by Egyptians bearing gifts of food and he watched it until the last child had passed. He shook his head at the emptiness of it all and continued towards Goshen. Their gods had been powerless in all of this and yet they still continued, at their Pharaoh's command, to rely on them. Moses wondered how many of those people still believed in the power of what they were doing. How many were just too scared of Pharaoh to disobey. He'd never know.

When Moses arrived in Goshen, his anger had mutated into a profound sadness for what would come about. He knew that it was not his fault; that Pharaoh had chosen this, but he almost could not bear the torment. Couldn't they just leave? He dropped down onto a rock, where he sat stunned and numb. He had to pull himself together. He had Israel to guide and lead now. Egypt was at the mercy of Pharaoh's leadership choices. Moses sat, staring out over the Israelite people. He was gathering his strength for the coming challenges, which he knew would be greater than anything else they'd experienced. A phrase drifted into his mind. He couldn't dislodge the thought. He knew it was the voice of God.

'Israel is *my* son, *my* firstborn.'

Part five

Repercussions

Chapter 34:

Ten

In the stillness of the Egyptian night, the streets were empty and quiet. In residences throughout the city, families slept. Their servants slept. The only sound came from the breeze gently rippling the surface of the Nile and causing the now bare branches to scratch against one another. Darkness blanketed the city.

Khaldun was sleeping in his own room in the impressive house by the river. He'd drifted off listening to the pleasant sound of lapping waves and feeling comfortable between his fresh linen sheets. He awoke suddenly. Until that moment, he'd been perfectly peaceful. Now he leant forward in his bed, propped up on his arms and looked cautiously around. His limbs were weak and his eyelids still felt heavy. But his chest was heaving with rapid shallow breaths and his heart was pumping blood faster than ever before. His eyes darted and his thoughts raced. What had woken him? He was certain he hadn't been dreaming. If he had, he couldn't remember any of it. He didn't remember hearing a noise either. There was nobody here. His room was dark and still. As his eyes adjusted to the light, he swung his legs soundlessly to one side, out of the sheets and slid down from the frame until his feet touched the cold floor. He tiptoed uneasily across the room, arms outstretched to find his way. He checked back over his shoulder. He shuddered. An unsettling feeling hung on him, as though someone was in his room. He knew he was alone, but he didn't feel it. Who was watching him? His fingertips rested on the window ledge and he leaned cautiously forward. He could make out the motion of ripples on the Nile. Dark ribbons flickering across a black surface. They were strangely intriguing. He watched for a while, momentarily forgetting his nerves. But his reverie was soon shattered. He remembered why he was out of bed and his fearful eyes drifted back to the street beneath him. Khaldun peered out of the window. He couldn't focus clearly. It was dark and everything looked a little more blurry and sinister than usual. But there was one shadowy shape that held his attention much longer. What was that? Whatever it was, he couldn't place it. It wasn't usually there. He was certain he'd never seen it before. His eyes widened. An icy whirlwind spiralled along the street, invisible yet strangely clear. Khaldun shuddered violently. He staggered backward as the shadow drifted towards his window. A cold pain struck him hard in the chest and he clutched at his heart. His scream echoed in the large room and seemed to continue long after his torpid body hit the floor.

Dudimose crept into Ibiya's room. He had a really bad feeling in the pit of his stomach and he hadn't slept. As he tiptoed across the floor, he noticed his hands were shaking. A trickle of sweat ran over his temple. He was more frightened now than he'd ever been in his life. Moses' threat had shaken him badly. His words tortured Dudimose: 'from the firstborn of Pharaoh who sits on his throne...'.

Dudimose knew he'd been stupid. Stubborn, short-sighted, foolish, arrogant, callous – he couldn't deny any of it. But only with this last act of utter recklessness had he begun to actually despise himself. He couldn't explain what had... didn't even recognise him... hadn't meant this to end... like... He leaned over Ibiya and let out a shudder. His knees buckled. He gasped for breath. His shaking hand flew to his mouth. He was struck by an overwhelming sensation in his chest. Ibiya's chest rose and fell smoothly. He was breathing. Asleep. Alive.

Crumpled on the floor next to his son's bed, Dudimose wept. Relief mixed with a deluge of guilt, remorse, self-hatred, pity and disgust. Not knowing what to think or feel anymore, Dudimose gave in completely to the raw emotion.

Umayma's chest was heaving. Her breaths were shallow and she was burning up. Something had woken her. Was she ill? She peered through the darkness, unable to see much. She could hear from their deep, rhythmic breathing that Pili and Sagira were both still sleeping peacefully. She didn't feel nauseous. Perhaps she'd just been uncomfortable. She rubbed her face. Gradually she calmed down and felt her temperature return to normal. She slowly closed her eyes again. But Umayma couldn't sleep. She still felt nervous, edgy. Something was wrong. Without moving, she opened her eyes again, stared through the dark room and listened hard. Silence, eerie silence. Umayma felt somebody's eyes on her.

'Pili?' she whispered. There was no reply. 'Are you awake?' Still nothing. Slowly, she sat up. Beside her, she could see two shapes, one much smaller than the other, tucked up and sleeping. If her sisters were both asleep, who was watching her? Umayma slipped out of bed and took a tentative step toward the window. She was shaky. She thought about waking Pili first – she'd feel better with her sister there – but decided against it. She was being silly. She just needed to have a quick look outside to reassure herself and then she'd be able to sleep again. There was no point waking anyone. Umayma took a deep breath and stuck her head outside the window. She gasped as something swiftly spiralled toward her, howling like the wind and a dark shadow drifted through her chest. Pain immediately ripped through her body. She reached out, clasping at the air. Her insides were cold as ice. She screamed a piercing scream.

No more tears would flow for Dudimose. Gradually he stopped sobbing and became aware of himself again. He was slumped on the floor, a shivering wreck. He was cold. He pitied himself. But he had nobody to blame. With a sniff, Dudimose sat up and wiped his cheeks with the dusty palms of his hands. He rubbed his arms to warm them and then pushed himself to his feet. He walked slowly towards a chair. He would sit in it all night if he had to. He wouldn't leave Ibiya's side. Not for... Dudimose felt eyes boring into his back. Fear immediately gripped his heart. Someone was watching him. Who was in the room? He spun round, ready to disarm the intruder, to defend his son. Nobody was there. He stayed alert.

'Dad?' Ibiya's drowsy voice broke the tension.

'Son, I...'

'What are you doing...?'

'I... I don't...'

Like sand driven across the desert by the wind, a rushing sound wound towards them. Dudimose's eyes were drawn to the doorway. Ibiya's were suspicious. The sound swelled as it swirled around corners and surged along the corridors. Its motion was swift and targeted.

Unstoppable. A whirlwind burst into Ibiya's room and rapidly engulfed it. The sound of cascading water circled and then slowly died away. Dudimose was unnerved. He was disorientated. Then realisation hit him and he panicked. Ibiya! He spun round and threw his arms wide. He staggered. His mouth fell open. He stared. A shadowy figure hovered in the air between him and his firstborn. Its dark, grey form was indistinct. Wisps of ethereal substance circled slowly, hanging in the air, obscuring Dudimose's view of his son.

There were no facial features. It wore no particular expression. It was merely a haze. And yet, something about the way it lurked made its purpose perfectly clear. The shadow moved towards Dudimose. It crept almost imperceptibly through the darkness. Dudimose felt it closing in on him. He backed away until his arms made contact with the wall. He flattened himself against it. There was nowhere else to go. Total darkness surrounded him. Time seemed to slow, so that Dudimose's thoughts became harrowingly clear. He hated himself. He hated everything he'd become. He wished fervently that he could change what he'd done, but he knew he couldn't. And now he knew he was too cowardly even to try to prevent this. The shadow turned to face Ibiya. Looking back at his son, Dudimose longed to change positions. Tears stung his eyes. He would gladly die to give his son the future he'd dreamed of.

Any future. Billows of dark, feathery silhouette trailed behind the shadow as it swooped across the empty space and struck Ibiya directly in the heart.

Rasui was awake. It was the middle of the night and he found himself, once again, unable to relax enough to stay asleep. Ever since his first day at work, he'd been sleeping in snatches. As soon as his eyes rolled back under his eyelids and his sleep deepened, the serpent would be there – vivid, real, terrifying. And once that happened he didn't stand a chance of getting back to sleep. He'd think about Pharaoh weeping in the hail and wonder again where this was heading. Would he regain strength enough to fight this or was the whole of Egypt careering around like a chariot with no driver, heading for self-destruction? He knew he should talk to someone about all this. He had to get it off his chest before the pressure made him ill, but he couldn't bear to do it. His parents were unfailingly loyal to Pharaoh. They'd never believe... and it would break their hearts. And Kepi... poor Kepi. For what it was worth, he would have confided in Kepi. He felt his heart in his mouth and tears welling up in the corners of his eyes. He still felt responsible for his sister's death. She'd insisted on coming to look for him in the hailstorm and nobody had been able to stop her. Why had she been so stupid? His mother had had to stay with the little ones and his father had not been able to restrain her. She'd wriggled and writhed and fought her way out of his grasp, insisting that she could look after herself. But she couldn't... not out there on her own. Rasui clenched his fists in anger. He wiped the tears from his cheek and navigated his way carefully over the sleeping bodies of his parents and siblings. He needed some space.

He climbed to the roof and stood at the edge, looking out. He wanted the old Egypt back. The one where everything had worked as it should – reliably and efficiently – and where Rasui had been carefree. He felt a sudden cold overwhelm him. Someone was there. Kepi? As soon as the thought entered his head, he felt stupid. But he just couldn't get used to... Then who was it? Who else was on the roof with him? He spun round and came face-to-face with a wispy, dark, intangible form. He involuntarily tensed. He stood staring. The moment lingered. Everything was still and quiet and surreal. Adrenaline pumped through his body. A swirling wind swept along the street below him and the shadow struck. He bent double, shuddering and shaking in agony. He was aware of saliva dribbling from his lips as a contraction gripped his heart. A tormented scream escaped before his chest tightened and his final breath expired. The tension finally released his body. The lifeless mass crumpled, hung momentarily over the edge of the roof and then fell. Rasui's body struck the ground outside his house as the whirlwind disappeared out of sight.

A scream broke into Dudimose's thoughts. Ibiya was screaming. It was excruciating; torturous. He'd never heard anything so loud and agonising. It struck him deep at the core of his being like a knife being slowly inserted, twisting and slicing him apart. And it was coming from his own flesh and blood. His firstborn son. The scream echoed from the walls of the room, long and loud. Similar screams joined from within the palace in a shocking discord. Then more screams joined the cacophony. The sound resonated in Dudimose's head. He clasped his ears. He bent double. He needed to shut out this sound; this wailing, lamenting, last anguished cry of a nation. His broken nation.

As the tension in Ibiya's body left him, Dudimose knew without a doubt he had achieved the only thing he'd ever wanted: to be a Pharaoh that would be remembered for generations. He also knew overpoweringly that he would be remembered in the worst conceivable way. He looked at his son. Ibiya had been handsome, tall. His face had beautiful features and a distinguished quality in the way it was constructed. Dudimose imagined the look gracing a statue. His heart broke to know that could never happen.

Ibiya's head flopped back limply. His arm fell from the bed. Dudimose gently picked it up and rested it on his son's torso. He leaned in close, cradled his firstborn and whispered in his ear, 'I'm so sorry, Ibiya; my son. I love you.'

Chapter 35:

The firstborn

Rasui's family poured out onto the street. His father fell to his knees. His mother stood screaming. Brothers and sisters clung to each other, staring and sobbing and shaking. His leg was broken and twisted at an unnatural angle. His skin was damp with perspiration and a look of shock remained, marring his young features. Agonising cries ruptured out from deep within Rasui's mother. Her raw grief was unbearable to listen to, terrible, aching, mournful tones. Cracked and broken between sobs. His father leant forward and gently closed Rasui's eyelids before putting his arms around her.

Pili caught Umayma's body as it fell. The scream had woken her and she'd leapt up and scrambled across the room before she'd even really woken. Her awareness seemed to catch up with the rest of her body as she struggled to lower Umayma's heavy torso to the ground. Pili watched her eyes turn glassy and her limbs fall limply to her sides. She screamed and buried her face in her hands. What had happened to her sister? She felt a reassuring hand on her shoulder. She heard Sagira beside her, calling 'Mayma, Mayma', and her father's urgent instructions to her mother. She was aware of her parents' busy movement around her but she couldn't remove her hands from her eyes. She didn't want to see. Didn't want to have to believe this was real. She was shaking. She couldn't stop screaming. Soon Sagira was screaming. Then all the chaotic movement stopped and her parents finally gave in to their sorrow. The four huddled together and wailed with the shock and injustice of their loss.

Khaldun's body lay expressionless on the cold, hard floor. The echoes of his scream were slowly fading. A servant entered and silently took in the scene. With a deep sigh and a little whimper he steeled himself for the task. He lifted Khaldun, cradling him like a baby, and laid his body on the bed. He arranged his arms, closed his eyelids, and covered him with a sheet. He stood a moment, as if to consider his next move, and then turned away and walked out of the room. Miw-Sher slunk in through the servant's legs as he pulled the door shut, and sprung up onto the bed. She nuzzled Khaldun's side and pawed at his chest. When she got no response she sat stiffly beside him.

Downstairs, the sympathetic words of the servant gave way first to his mother's indignation and distress, then to his father's angry heartbreak. Their misery resounded in the large room. Upstairs, Miw-Sher alone sat with her Khaldun, adding her own feline screeching and wailing to the growing lament.

Egypt's streets were still blanketed in darkness, but the silence had been shattered by the lament of a nation. In every household on every street, somebody had died. Many households had lost multiple members from different generations. A mournful, disharmonious gut-wrenching roar, like a lion maimed, rose up and drifted on the breeze. Nothing had been heard in Egypt before to rival its irrepressible horror.

At the gates of the palace, a growing crowd of angry residents was hurling abuse at Pharaoh. They were hurt, they were incensed, and they were looking for answers. Pharaoh had let them all down. He had not prevented this, the worst of atrocities ever to afflict Egypt and now, when they needed him most, he had failed to make an appearance. The metal gates clanked loudly as the mass shook them brutally against their fixings. Some were scaling their heights, desperate to get into the courtyard. Not a single guard or servant was preventing them. The palace seemed abandoned. Where was Pharaoh? What was he doing? Why wasn't he here? The first man to reach the top swung a leg over the top of the gate and lowered his feet to locate a foothold for his descent. A cheer erupted and a new wave of climbers, encouraged by the battle cry, leapt and scrambled onto the thick metal bars. They were going to storm the palace and find the man who was responsible for all this. And they would have their revenge.

Dudimose heard the angry yelling as he staggered through the colonnade, cradling Ibiya's cold, lifeless body. He was overwhelmed with fear when he heard the stampede of citizens coming over the gate. They'd kill him. He struggled on, careering from side to side like a drunken man with the combination of grief and utter exhaustion. He battled on and emerged onto his podium to see his people angrily streaming across his courtyard toward the steps. He knew he was going to die now, and he wanted to do it here, with his firstborn son, in his favourite spot in all of Egypt. Tears streaming down his wretched face, he looked across the city at the sun rising into position. The shouting abated. The crowd stood still. But he didn't notice. Dudimose shook as he watched the sun emerge over the tip of his pyramid. He watched the obelisk light up. His falcon cast into silhouette. He steadfastly concentrated on the spectacular view he'd created, determined this should be the last thing he ever saw, and he waited. He waited for the moment when the cold blade of a sword would pierce his chest, or he'd be hauled down the steps and left to the mercy of the angry crowd. He squeezed

Ibiya's corpse close to his chest. But the crowd's anger was melting. They stood in shock. The heir was dead. Pharaoh had experienced their loss firsthand and he'd reacted just like the rest of them. Their King was demonstrating real, human emotion in a way they'd never seen before. One by one, people sank to their knees and sobbed. They cried for their own losses. And they cried with Pharaoh. The moment Dudimose was waiting for never came.

Chapter 36:

Go!

Moses laughed out loud. He couldn't help himself. It was a moment of perfect relief in the tension and stress of everything he knew he had to achieve now. The first Israelites, a group of women, staggered back across the border into Goshen. They were accompanied by several giggling children. The women and older children carried heavy armfuls of clothing, made from the most exquisite and beautiful linen. It was the finer sort, most often worn by Egyptian nobility. The smaller children wore as many golden necklaces, anklets and bracelets as they could bear the weight of. Even the youngest, still tottering along, had rings on her fingers and other precious little items in the basket she carried. The group chattered and laughed, unable to believe their success.

'They just gave it all to us!' One called out.

Another joined in. 'They insisted. They wanted us to have it.'

Moses smiled at their obvious delight. These people had suffered for so long under the supervision of the same Egyptians who had just gladly given them their most treasured possessions. The depth of the Egyptians' change of heart was unexpected. But that was what made it so delicious. Moses was pleased with Israel. They'd had to wait so long for God to deliver what he'd promised them, but they'd followed their instructions exactly. They had gone back over the border into Egypt one last time and requested these items. And they'd been granted them. They'd also carefully carried out everything he'd asked of them before the final horrific plague. Not one of Israel's firstborn numbered among the dead, because they had faithfully smeared blood on their doorposts and lintels as a sign. They had stayed inside, killed and prepared their lamb. He was proud of them all.

'Go home,' he called out to them. 'Pack your belongings. We do not have long.'

The women looked up from their animated conversations and nodded solemnly. They understood how serious this was. They gathered the children, who were performing an accomplished parody of Egyptian nobility, and hurried away.

Moses stayed a little longer to watch as more and more of his people returned. He saw the treasures they had despoiled – riches beyond anything he'd seen since his childhood in an Egyptian palace – but still found himself unable to comprehend the scale and importance of what was happening. The scene seemed unreal – beyond what his human mind could explain. Laughter was the only reaction he could find. Finally, he tore himself away. He had work to do.

A tower of brilliant orange fire erupted above Moses. He stood perfectly still, holding his arms wide so that those immediately behind him would do the same. It was the most spectacular thing he'd ever seen. The burning bush phenomenon, which had rendered him awestruck at the time, seemed a little pathetic in comparison. Flames spiralled and roared fiercely upwards in a column that lit up the entire sky. The heat they exuded was overwhelming; the light too bright to look at directly. Moses was awestruck. He'd recently seen lightning and hail, lethal in its ferocity, a snake that outsized and out-manoeuvred the competition without apparent effort, and water that became blood on command. But this miracle was different. It had the element of pure, virtuous beauty that each of those other things had lacked. God's pillar of fire was not here to challenge an oppressor's misplaced belief. This was a generous provision for his own people. Trudging across a bleak and difficult landscape; transporting everyone from children to the most elderly Israelites; leading animals and laden with provisions, this journey would have been rendered impossible after nightfall. The light provided by the spectacular shifting inferno meant that every rock, every dune, every obstacle on the ground was plainly visible. The massive temperature drop at night was no longer a concern for Moses and the column would continue to guide them as the cloud had done in the day. Moses had many doubts and questions about what lay ahead on this journey, but he could not doubt God's sincerity, ability or his presence with his people. He had freed them from Egypt – every single individual. He looked back at the long line of Israelite families making their way across the near barren landscape. It continued back as far as the horizon. How would he feed all these people? Where would they rest? They'd put their confidence in Moses and he felt responsible for every single one of them. With a deep breath, he faced the flame again and strode into its light, grateful that he was just a messenger.

Chapter 37:

Pursuit

Dudimose's feet were planted firmly on the plate of his chariot. His weight was distributed over the axle, leaving the horse unburdened by his weight, free to achieve the maximum possible speed. He hadn't wasted time attaching the leather-covered wood panels at the sides and back. He wasn't anticipating a need to defend himself against a counter-attack. That idea was laughable. Israel was not an army. Not even close. A bow was slung over his shoulder and a quiver of arrows hung over the rear corners of the chariot. At the front, he also had a sheath of javelins if circumstances necessitated their use. He was ready.

His blood boiled as he reminded himself how much the Israelites had plundered. He could not bear the audacity of them to so blatantly insult him after he'd granted them their freedom. And after everything else their people had cost him. He felt a surge of anger pump through his body, energising him. Dudimose felt more alive at this moment than at any time since before Ibiya's death. He inhaled the cool air and bellowed his command. His voice lingered in the air. Beside and behind him, he felt the reassuring presence of his most skilful archers, and behind them, the rest of his army and the extra chariots bearing his runners. He was bringing the entire force of Egypt to pay back Moses for everything. He felt powerful, commanding and more than justified. Dudimose was back where he belonged.

The two beautiful, powerful horses who would be carrying Dudimose into battle took their first steps. The six-spoke wheels began to turn smoothly beneath Dudimose's feet, their bronze rims silencing the movement to give the maximum possible level of stealth. Dudimose raised his fist into the air as his driver whipped the horses and they accelerated away, leading his army into the night. The air passed swiftly over Dudimose's skin, refreshing and exhilarating him. The design of the chariot smoothed out the rough bumps of the desert landscape and the galloping rise and fall of the horses, but the movement of the wheels still travelled through his legs and body. His posture was constantly responding to the motion. He felt alive.

Dudimose did not need to direct his army. The Israelites had made an easy target of themselves with that burning tower of light that led them. His army simply aimed towards it. They could not possibly fail to catch up with three million Israelites travelling on foot. It made the chase much less exciting for him. He sighed. Couldn't they even get that right? Although, he thought, it was also less stressful – this felt like a training exercise. It was going to be the easiest mission his army had ever experienced. They'd be home by sunrise.

The pace slowed as Dudimose allowed time for his army to fall back into a narrower formation. They were approaching a gorge, a massive split in a towering rock face, where the Israelites had disappeared. Dudimose sent five of his sharpest shooters in ahead of himself. Five seemed enough, more than adequate for the job. It was only sensible to afford himself a little protection, just in case. He really didn't anticipate needing it, but... you can never be too careful. He followed at a slight distance. They had slowed to a walking pace because the twisting path meant that the Israelite's fire was temporarily out of their line of sight. With the walls of this crevice towering above them, darkness overpowered them. Dudimose grinned. This was more of an adventure. The air was slightly dank and musty. It tasted odd whenever he inhaled. Drivers struggled to keep their pairs of horses calm and quiet, reassuring them and guiding them on. Wheels bumped their way over rocks and potholes. Dudimose was thrown around on his platform. He adjusted his stance to better withstand the jolting. He was impressed how well the bronze rimmed wheels were coping. Even in this potentially echoing environment, they were relatively quiet. If only the horses were as reliable. They'd never trained in such claustrophobic conditions. Dudimose made a mental note to address that before future missions. Another time it could be more important that the horses perform immaculately.

The channel widened slightly. Dudimose's chariot sped up and cornered smoothly around the bend. Then his driver brought his horses to an abrupt halt. Dudimose was thrown forward. The horses fought back. The animals in front had reared up on their hind legs. One was trying to sidestep, dragging its partner reluctantly with it and dangerously tilting the chariot. The archer leapt clear and waited nervously in a hollow crevice in the wall. All ten horses were whinnying and shying. One turned itself completely around, breaking free of its yolk and, realising that it was trapped between the rest of the army and the fiery pillar, was trying to bolt. It reared up again and kicked out hard. Dudimose ducked. His own horses were still fighting hard against the driver. His heart started to beat faster. He was close. He could almost feel the presence of Israel, but what was his next move? He couldn't fire arrows at a column of burning air. He couldn't go back – the rest of the army was still piling into the crevice behind him. And all around him rapidly increasing chaos threatened his attack as the horses reacted against the heat, the glare and the sheer eeriness of the situation.

Chapter 38:

Demise

The water raged. Great billowing waves circled and crashed on either side of Moses. Although there was a significant clear distance on either side of him where the water did not encroach, the ebbing and flowing, eddying and breaking was deeply unnerving. Moses was sweating. His palms were clammy. He strode purposefully onwards through the intra-tidal path. It was seemingly never-ending. His pace had an urgency about it that had not been present on this journey until now. His features were focused. If the water itself were not disconcerting enough, he knew that the full force of the Egyptian army was closer to them now than the ever-present servant was at all times to his Pharaoh. They were being held back only by the swirling mass of flame in the narrow gorge. Moses did not know why they had followed. He did not know how many had come in pursuit. He did not even know what they intended to do. Had they driven Israel out of Egypt in order to slaughter them in the desert? They were weak, tired and defenceless. It would be a massacre. Moses knew beyond a doubt that God was still demonstrating his superior power. He knew it in theory. But he didn't feel it. Pharaoh had brought his physical might and high-tech vehicles to demonstrate his power. God was providing a supernatural way out from a dead-end. Just when the people had given up all hope of escape and given in to total despair, Moses had used his staff and God had literally lifted the surface of the water high into the air and ripped it in two, repelling the two halves apart. He was holding back their pursuers with another supernatural phenomenon. Moses did not have to rely on what his senses understood to explain the situation. But he couldn't help it.

All the messages in his mind were telling him that he was in a very dangerous predicament. If the sea didn't first plunge in and sweep them all away, then the army were certain to. Everything in his body told him to move – fast. And that's exactly what he was doing. His heart racing and puffing hard, Moses forged ahead. He hoped that the rest of his nation was able to keep up with the pace. He needed to get to the opposite bank of the Red Sea and find a route where horses could not follow, or a place where three million people and all their livestock could be hidden. Even as he strove relentlessly towards this goal, he knew in his heart how futile it was. Hiding Israel would be impossible, and finding obstacles to impede Pharaoh's army was improbable enough to be ruled out altogether. His army knew the land here better than anyone, certainly better than Moses. But what other option did he have? He prayed aloud as he strode forward. He needed a miracle, another miracle. He couldn't do this alone. Please rescue us. You've brought us this far. Don't let us die now.

* * *

Dudimose issued the command to push forward. The fire had eventually moved from the opening in the cliff face and his army had now repositioned themselves and their horses. His original strategy remained. The army would focus exclusively on hunting Moses. Once he'd been dealt with and his staff shattered, the rest of the Israelites would be much more compliant. As Dudimose's horse galloped, dragging the reluctant chariot wheels through the sand, he surveyed the scene. Two, apparently solid, walls of water stood high on either side of the trail of Israelites. Pharaoh could only assume this was another of their god's interventions. He was determined that this would be the one that let them all down. Dudimose had the force of his entire army at his command. He would win this time. He felt his impatience grow as the sand slowed their progress. But it only fuelled his desire even more. He was angry. He was impatient. And he was more focused on this one goal than anything he'd achieved until now. Moses would be leading. He'd already be at the other end of this supernatural channel. That meant they needed to move. Fast. He approached the solid bed of the Red Sea, bracing himself for speeding up, but his body was hit by a powerful wind. Dudimose strained forward against it. The horses were working as hard as possible, but their speed was undoubtedly being compromised. They looked astounding, racing through the waves, the wind billowing through their manes. Their power was unquestionable. Could they gallop even faster? Dudimose wanted to find out. His impatient ambition drove him to risk everything in pursuit of Moses. He bellowed his command and grinned to himself as the rushing waves whistled past him on either side, and the gap between his army and the Israelites began to close.

★ ★ ★

Moses stood on the bank of the Red Sea, nervously jiggling his foot. He was willing the thin trail of stragglers on. They seemed to be moving so slowly and the Egyptians so quickly, gaining ground fast. The horses galloped through the waves at terrifying speed and Moses knew the Israelites would not hear them approach. They were still too far away to hear his warnings either, so all he could do was watch in horror. Six horses, side by side, moved in perfect unison with their manes flowing. They resembled a wave rolling forwards from the horizon, rising and falling in smooth, arcing motion. Moses glanced at the few remaining Israelites. They hardly seemed to be any closer than before. He grasped his staff tightly in his right hand. He could now see the archers standing tall on their platforms, bows raised. Beyond them a second wave of equestrian strength and power. Moses saw one of the Israelites nudge another and look back over his shoulder. He saw them point. He saw their horrified faces turn back towards him and watched as they broke into a run. He watched a father sweep up a small child. Two men support a frail woman. He saw spirit, determination and incredible selfless bravery. But they were still in imminent danger. His fist tightened around his staff. His eyes locked onto the front row of Egyptian horses, mentally calculating the remaining time. He wasn't convinced they would outrun the horses.

★ ★ ★

Dudimose had tunnel vision now. He was intently focused on the other side of the Red Sea and the form of Moses standing on the shore. He narrowed his eyes at the sight of that abominable piece of wood and willed himself closer. Sights and sounds rushed past him but Dudimose was oblivious. He had blocked out everything except his target and the voice of his own body. The pounding of his heart echoed the beat of the horses' hooves. His shallow breaths excited him. The adrenaline racing around his body and the anticipation of what he was about to achieve made the hairs on his arms stand on end. Dudimose would not allow history to remember him as the pharaoh who allowed Egypt to fall apart around him. His actions today were writing a better version. He could visualise the engraved pylons now: images of horses and chariots, archers riding through the waves, captured slaves, and Dudimose triumphantly leading them all. Dudimose would ensure today that he'd eternally be remembered as the man who daringly rescued Egypt from the brink of disaster, who hunted an oppressor and plunderer, took a nation of thieves back into slavery and rebuilt Egypt; bigger, better and stronger than ever before. Ibiya may never inherit Egypt now, but that didn't mean Dudimose was going to let it crumble. He had a reputation to regain.

★ ★ ★

Moses' eyes widened. The walls of water collapsed in an instant. Vast quantities of liquid rushed down like a waterfall to fill the void. Horses were swept off their feet like papyrus in a breeze. Soldiers were dragged down with the current. They were unable to fight the sheer power of the cascade. The water swirled and churned, holding them down. Screams were made mute by the pounding of the two bodies of water as they tangled and wrestled their way down. Limbs waved momentarily above the surface before their valiant efforts were overwhelmed. Moses stood in awe, side by side with the few whose lives had been spared by mere moments; staff outstretched over the Red Sea. He watched the surface rise and fall with the swell; the waves subside gradually. He imagined the torrent still raging beneath the calm surface; the tortured, twisted expressions on the faces; the tearing pain of the battering impacts; the dwindling consciousness as water infiltrated the airways. He didn't want to see this. He wished his thoughts would stop; wished that he could turn away.

* * *

Torrents of water battered Dudimose from all directions. He was immersed abruptly into total darkness. His limbs were being yanked, shoved and dragged painfully around his contorting body by the currents. He was stunned, too shocked to react. He struggled to comprehend what was happening to him. Where were his army? Where was his chariot? His thrilling chase had been interrupted; ripped from him in an instant and he felt as though he was falling. Everything was black. Was this what dying was like? Had the horses thrown him off? Why couldn't he remember? Suddenly he came to his senses. He was in the water! Dudimose swirled around. He wasn't certain which way was up. His head was spinning with the tumultuous currents and pressure pounded his insides. He felt sharp pain in his nose and eyes and panicked. He'd instinctively held his breath. But he suspected he'd inhaled water in the process. The thought panicked him. Dudimose's limbs flailed around, jerking, lurching and circling, as he contemplated his new reality. He forced himself to focus and kick. His legs felt heavy, weak. But somehow he kept kicking. He found a rhythm and felt his body finally propel itself into motion, but he couldn't tell whether he was travelling towards the surface, or further down. He was disorientated and scared. Something heavy and hard struck Dudimose's back. Pain spread down his spine and legs. He felt the object pressing down on him, dragging him down. He didn't have the strength to push it off. He dived down and out to one side, kicking off the object and turned to watch the spokes of the chariot wheel move past his face and fade into the murkiness. He tumbled over and kicked hard away from it. This must be up. Fighting against the pull of the sinking chariot, he kicked and pulled with all his remaining strength. He needed to breathe. He had to be fast. He felt himself being dragged down and kicked faster. Every instinct now was telling him to exhale. He pushed his lips harder together to keep his mouth closed. His legs were tiring. He sculled through the water, relying more on the strength of his arms. Dudimose saw light pervading the dark waters at the same moment his reflex to breathe activated without his permission. His jaw opened wide. Water gushed into his mouth, gagging him. He tried to cough it up, but only managed to take on more water. He closed his mouth and tried to swallow, but his throat was constricting. He screamed silently beneath the surface as pain wrenched his body apart. Dudimose's limbs had become limp and unresponsive. He stared helplessly at the light above him, unable to find the final burst of strength to propel him to safety. The light faded as Egypt's Pharaoh drifted into unconsciousness. An undertow dragged his body downwards. Moments later, Dudimose's heart executed its final beat.

★ ★ ★

The lapping waves at the shoreline deposited the first body. Hollow eyes stared emptily at the sky. Limbs contorted at grotesque angles. Once handsome features were distorted by waterlogged skin and tinged blue. Along the shoreline, more bodies drifted up and rested on the ground. The waves unceremoniously unloaded the foreign material. Israel watched in silence. A horrified, awestruck, uncomprehending silence settled in.

Israel is safe, Moses told himself over and over again. He was waiting for the significance to sink in. *It's over.*

Dudimose is dead. Moses felt that he should say something profound to mark the moment, but no words came to mind. He was torn between two deep emotions; great sadness for the cost of the past months, and immense relief that God had delivered Israel from Egypt as he'd promised. It was not the journey Moses would have chosen, but they were here. God had been faithful to his word.

Moses knew Israel would expect him to say something now. He opened his mouth to address them, wondering what he could say. But what came out was more eloquent than any speech he could have prepared. Moses found himself singing. Something inside his heart was expressing itself – 'This is my God, and I will praise him.'

EPILOGUE

Dudimose was not present to witness the final horrific insult unfolding.

If he had been, he would have been mortified to see the fate of his masterpiece. All that remained of the temple he'd planned and overseen was a massive pile of rubble. Within the heap, large chunks of columns and statues remained intact. They protruded at odd angles, giving a glimpse of the wonder that should have graced this spot. Instead, plaster, brick and precious metal lay coated in a thick layer of dust. On the other side of the Nile, Pharaoh's pyramid, the final resting place he had created for himself, stood empty. His coffin had not been closed. His body, neither embalmed nor mummified, was forever lost to the Red Sea. The pyramid should have been his lasting monument. Instead, this is the place all of Egypt now visited to lament him. Rather than his loss, they mourned his choices and the course he had chosen for them. Someone had climbed to the top of this heap and balanced the head of one of Pharaoh's broken statues there. His image lived on alongside the wreckage; the visible symbol of his foolishness.

Neither was Ibiya.

Egypt's heir had not stood a chance. The firstborn prince had shown great promise as the future ruler of the civilisation. He had an instinctive grasp of moral concerns, an empathy with his people and courage to challenge whatever issues he saw. His training should have built on that foundation, preparing him for the whole scope of responsibilities and challenges he would face. Instead, it attacked that core, leaving him helpless to impact the nation for good. His mature voice was drowned out by his father's stubborn insistence. Ibiya's work was obstructed, criticised and ultimately sentenced to failure. His future was risked in a game with the highest possible stakes. His father lost. Egypt lost. Ibiya's young life was sacrificed.

They had been caught entirely off guard.

A man sat outside his door in a residential street in Egypt. His family were mourning their firstborn. Like everyone else, he had suffered bereavement. Sons, brothers, fathers and grandfathers had died in one terrible night. The sense of grief overwhelmed him, and his community. He stared blankly out at the street between volatile periods of sobbing. At times he'd feel a hand on his shoulder or a friend sitting beside him. At other moments he felt totally, abysmally alone. Normality had been put on hold while the nation came to terms with what had happened. Its old identity had been destroyed, but a new one had not yet been created. The people were held together only by their wordless sense of shared loss. A thriving metropolis had become a poverty-stricken, wreck of a home. Food was scarce. Livelihoods had been destroyed. The religious beliefs that had underpinned every detail of their lives had been undermined and now they were left with a void – a gaping void. The man's eyes were glazed. His heart was heavy. His soul ached for healing. For everybody, this was a time of reflection; of looking inwards, a time of learning, consoling and slowly, painstakingly, reluctantly accepting. The foreigners' arrival was like a knife in the back of a sleeping child. They had not seen it coming. The possibility was not even considered.

The world's greatest civilisation was vulnerable and exposed. Egypt was defenceless.

Egypt had nothing resembling a defence. The world's strongest, best-trained, best-equipped army which they once boasted had been entirely decimated. Every soldier, chariot, horse and weapon had been dispatched in pursuit of Moses and his people. The waters of the Red Sea had consumed them with one great swallow.

The army met its demise as one complete unit. The shattered population they left behind were still lost, hurt and confused. Not yet ready to leave their houses; much less convene to install a new system of defence. The grieving citizens were left vulnerably exposed.

A society that had already lost so much had now also lost its heart.

The man sat on his doorstep reflecting. He had done little else for days. How did he come to find himself in this position? he wondered, not for the first time today. How did the head of a respectable family, a scribe and champion spear fisherman, come to find himself hungry, tired and hollow? He was a mess of resentment, pain and humiliation. And then the foreigners arrived and took away the last remaining glimpse of hope in his desperately dark existence. They took away the common thread of Egyptian-ness that held the people together. They destroyed culture and religion and imposed their own ways of life. Ways that insulted everything he'd once believed in. The man closed his eyes. What was there left for him now? Being alive here was too painful to bear. He picked up his fishing spear and turned it slowly until the point was aligned with his heart. He counted to three, nodding each beat and drew it slowly back away from his torso. Swiftly, powerfully, he thrust it through his chest. His face contorted with pain as the blade edge travelled into his heart.

Egypt had just paid the price.

Note for the reader

The events depicted in *The Egyptian Nightmare* are based on the stories recorded in Exodus 5–15. The author has woven these stories together with historical and archeological evidence of life in Egypt to help you explore the difficult questions that the Bible text raises. No one is sure about the identity of the Pharaoh in Exodus, but the author has chosen Dudimose, who was the last Pharaoh of the 13th dynasty. Ibiya is a fictional name, but the Pharaoh of Exodus did have an heir. It is likely that only firstborn sons died in the tenth plague, but the author has included the story of a firstborn daughter too, to illustrate just how far-reaching the plagues were that hit Egypt.

Read the Bible passages about Moses and the Pharaoh and reflect on what they tell you about God. What is God saying to you through these stories? If you have any questions, find a Christian you trust and chat through your ideas, thoughts and concerns.

What are Dark Chapters?

What is the Christian response to the vast array of horror books aimed at young people? Is it to condemn these titles and ban them from our shelves? Is it to ignore this trend and let our young people get on with reading them? At Scripture Union, we believe this presents a fantastic opportunity to help young people get into the pages of God's Word and wrestle with some of the difficult questions of faith.

The text does not sensationalise the horrific aspects of each story for entertainment's sake, and therefore trivialise what the story has to say. On the contrary, each retold account uses the more fantastic and gruesome episodes of each character's story to grip the reader and draw them into assessing why these events take place.

The reader is asked throughout the books to consider questions about the nature of God, how we should live as Christians, what value we place on things of this world – power, wealth, influence or popularity – and what God values.

For additional information and resources, visit
www.scriptureunion.org.uk/darkchapters

Izevel, Queen of Darkness

Izevel fell, fell and fell. She looked frantically downwards.

Around her, with outstretched arms of flame, and pale, decaying, ghastly faces, were the beings she had loved to worship. And they were laughing; hideous, screaming laughter. In one despairing moment she realised, too late, that they had lied to her all her life and she had believed them. Her Nightmares had come to claim her for ever.

Slowly, slowly, slowly, Izevel, Princess of Tyre, works her influence over her new husband, Ahav, and his kingdom Israel. Leading them away from Adonai, she encourages the unspeakable practices of Baal worship. But despite her best efforts, the Lord and his prophets will not be disposed of so easily. Increasingly driven mad by her own lifestyle, Izevel races headlong towards her own grisly downfall.

978 1 84427 536 6
£5.99

The Sky Will Fall

The man's arms were outstretched and were placed firmly on the pillars at the centre of the temple. These pillars supported the whole roof of the temple. And it was an ornate roof, painted to resemble the sky. Despite being inside, the roof was painted to look like you were out in the open. Shennahgon looked at the roof – the sky – and began to see the cracks appear. Brick by brick and stone by stone, the sky began to fall.

Shimsom thought back over all he had achieved for the Lord. He was one of God's judges, appointed by the Lord to guide his people and rid them of Philistine rule. But Shimsom's methods – a donkey's jawbone, pairs of foxes and a Philistine marriage – had led him here, tied to pillars in the Temple of Dagon. But if he was going to meet a gruesome end, then he would take everyone else with him…

978 1 84427 537 3
£5.99